Campus Odyssey
A Journey Through Engineering Life

Swagat Mohanty

Ukiyoto Publishing

All global publishing rights are held by

Ukiyoto Publishing

Published in 2024

Content Copyright © Swagat Mohanty

ISBN 9789364944502

All rights reserved.
No part of this publication may be reproduced, transmitted, or stored in a retrieval system, in any form by any means, electronic, mechanical, photocopying, recording or otherwise, without the prior permission of the publisher.

The moral rights of the author have been asserted.

This is a work of fiction. Names, characters, businesses, places, events, locales, and incidents are either the products of the author's imagination or used in a fictitious manner. Any resemblance to actual persons, living or dead, or actual events is purely coincidental.

This book is sold subject to the condition that it shall not by way of trade or otherwise, be lent, resold, hired out or otherwise circulated, without the publisher's prior consent, in any form of binding or cover other than that in which it is published.

www.ukiyoto.com

ACKNOWLEDGEMENTS

With deep gratitude, I want to acknowledge the incredible people who have been a part of my journey in creating "Campus Odyssey." This book would not exist without the support and inspiration of so many.

To my friends from NIT Rourkela, thank you for being the heart and soul of my college experience. The memories we made together—late-night study marathons, countless cups of tea, laughter, and even the challenging moments—have profoundly shaped who I am today. Your friendship, honest feedback, and constant encouragement inspired me to write this story. This book is a reflection of all the experiences we shared, and I'm deeply grateful to each of you.

To my parents and sister, your constant support has been my anchor throughout this journey—thank you for always being there.

I also want to express my sincere appreciation to Ukiyoto Publishing. Your guidance and dedication have been instrumental in bringing this story to life. Thank you for believing in this project and helping me share it with the world.

Lastly, to everyone who has touched my life, even in the smallest ways, thank you. Whether you realize it or not, you've been a part of this journey. This book is for all of us—for the friendships, the lessons, and the unforgettable moments that make up our stories.

CONTENTS

Prologue: The Shelter of Comfort   1

- Introduction to Arjun and his pampered lifestyle.
- His close-knit family and the protective environment.
- Academic aspirations and the initial disappointment of missing out on IIT.

Chapter 1: Stepping Out   5

- The shock and realization of joining NIT.
- Farewell to family and the emotional departure from his hometown.
- First impressions of the college and hostel life.

Chapter 2: The New Environment   12

- Adjusting to the government college facilities.
- The culture shock of shared accommodations and common bathrooms.
- Initial struggles with the food and cleanliness.

Chapter 3: The Academic Pressure   19

- The intensity of engineering courses and the competitive atmosphere.
- Introduction to the professors and their teaching styles.
- Arjun's struggle to keep up with the coursework and assignments.

Chapter 4: Making Friends   26

- The challenge of breaking out of his shell to make new friends.
- The formation of his first friend group and the dynamics within.

- Bonding over late-night study sessions, shared meals, and hostel shenanigans.

Chapter 5: Ragging and Bonding — 34

- Introduction to the seniors: Nikhil, Archit, Akshay, and Prateek.
- Arjun and his friends being called to the senior hostel at 12 am for a ragging session.
- The ordeal of kneeling down, dancing, and enduring the gruelling four hours.
- Unexpected bonding and camaraderie developed with the seniors afterward.

Chapter 6: Extracurricular Activities — 41

- Discovering and joining various clubs and societies.
- Participation in technical festivals, cultural events, and sports.
- The importance of extracurriculars in personal growth and resume building.

Chapter 7: One-Sided Love — 45

- Arjun's initial friendship with a girl who seemed interested in him.
- Late-night chats and the excitement of first love.
- The realization that she loved a senior and the heartbreak that followed.
- Arjun's emotional struggle and eventual growth, emerging stronger.

Chapter 8: Love's Second Chance   49

- Navigating the complexities of romantic relationships in college.
- Balancing time between studies, friends, and a significant other.
- Lessons learned from heartbreaks and maintaining healthy relationships.

Chapter 9: Coping with Homesickness   56

- Episodes of homesickness and the emotional toll.
- Strategies Arjun uses to cope, such as calls home and visits during holidays.
- The role of friends and college activities in alleviating homesickness.

Chapter 10: Proxies and Hostel Friendship   62

- The culture of proxies in attendance and its risks.
- The camaraderie and trust developed among hostel mates.
- Late-night conversations, pranks, and the deep bonds formed.

Chapter 11: The Startup Challenge   67

- The initiation of a startup idea with friends.
- The challenges faced in the development and implementation.
- The experience of pitching to investors and industry professionals.

Chapter 12: The Midway Crisis   70

- The pressure of mid-semester exams and project deadlines.
- Overcoming a major academic setback and the subsequent self-reflection.

- Seeking help from mentors and peers to get back on track.

Chapter 13: The Night Canteen Chronicles　　　　76

- The night canteen as a sanctuary for students.
- Bonding with friends and seniors over late-night snacks and conversations.
- Memorable pranks and stories shared in the canteen.

Chapter 14: Internships and Industry Exposure　　81

- The hunt for summer internships and the application process.
- Experience working in the industry and the practical learning involved.
- Balancing internships with academic responsibilities.

Chapter 15: The Cultural Festival　　　　　　　　87

- Participation in the cultural festival and the vibrant atmosphere.
- Forming a band and performing at the festival.
- The camaraderie and new connections made during the event.

Chapter 16: The Inter-College Sports Extravaganza　92

- Participation in inter-college sports events.
- The spirit of competition and teamwork.
- Achievements and memories from the sports extravaganza.

Chapter 17: The Midnight Adventure　　　　　　95

- An adventurous exploration of a rumoured underground floor.
- The thrill and discoveries made during the midnight adventure.

- The bonding experience and lessons learned.

Chapter 18: Broken Friendships   100

- The strain on friendships due to misunderstandings, competition, and personal differences.
- A significant fallout with a close friend and its emotional impact.
- The process of dealing with betrayal, reconciliation attempts, and moving on.

Chapter 19: The Research Project   107

- The mandatory research project in the final year.
- Challenges faced in the development and implementation.
- Success and recognition gained from the project.

Chapter 20: Placement Preparations   112

- The intense preparation for campus placements.
- Practicing for interviews and refining resumes.
- The emotional rollercoaster of securing a job.

Chapter 21: The Final Year   116

- The bittersweet experience of the final year in college.
- Reflecting on the journey and personal growth over the years.
- The excitement and fear of entering the professional world.

Chapter 22: Graduation and Beyond   122

- The emotions of graduation day and saying goodbye to friends.
- Securing a job and the transition from student to professional.

- The realization of the importance of the NIT experience in shaping his future.

Epilogue: A New Chapter Begins   129

- Arjun's reflections on his journey from a pampered boy to a resilient young man.
- The lifelong friendships and memories made at NIT.
- Looking ahead to new challenges and opportunities with confidence.

About the Author   133

Prologue: The Shelter of Comfort

Arjun Mehra sat in the backseat of his father's sleek black Mercedes, the familiar hum of the engine and the cool air-conditioning providing a comforting cocoon against the chaos of Delhi's streets. He glanced out of the tinted window, watching the world blur past – a world he had always viewed from a distance, shielded by the privileges his family's wealth afforded him. The bustling markets, the crowded streets, the cacophony of honking horns – it was all a part of a city that felt both intimately familiar and strangely distant.

His thoughts were interrupted by the soft chime of his phone. A message from his best friend, Karan, flashed on the screen: "All set for the send-off party tonight? It's going to be epic!"

Arjun smiled, typing a quick reply. "Wouldn't miss it for the world." He knew tonight would be a night to remember, a grand farewell to the life he had known. The weight of his departure loomed over him, but he was determined to enjoy every moment with his friends and family before leaving.

As the car maneuvered through the heavy traffic, Arjun's mind wandered back to the day he received his JEE results. The initial thrill of securing a high rank was quickly overshadowed by the crushing disappointment of not making it to an IIT. His parents had reassured him that NIT was still a prestigious institution, but the sting of falling short of his ultimate goal lingered. He had always been the golden boy, excelling in academics and meeting every expectation. This was the first time he felt the bitter taste of failure.

The car slowed as they approached the towering gates of their home – a sprawling mansion nestled in one of the city's most exclusive neighbourhoods. As the gates swung open, Arjun's mother emerged from the house, her face lighting up with a smile that chased away his lingering doubts. She had always been his pillar of support, and her strong faith in him was a constant source of strength.

"There's my boy!" she exclaimed, enveloping him in a warm hug as he stepped out of the car. "How was your day, Son?"

"Good, Mom," Arjun replied, hugging her back. "Just wrapping up some last-minute stuff."

His father, a stern but loving figure, appeared at the doorway, nodding in approval. "Enjoy tonight, Arjun. You've worked hard. But remember, the real journey begins now."

Arjun nodded, feeling a mix of excitement and apprehension. He knew his father was right. Leaving the comfort of his home and stepping into the unknown world of NIT was a daunting prospect. But it was also an opportunity – a chance to prove himself, to forge his own path.

As the evening wore on, the send-off party reached its peak. Arjun found himself surrounded by friends and family, their laughter and well-wishes echoing around him. The garden was beautifully decorated with fairy lights, and the air was filled with the aroma of his favourite dishes. He moved from group to group, engaging in conversations, sharing memories, and trying to soak in every moment.

Yet, amid the celebration, he felt a pang of uncertainty. Would he be able to cope with the challenges that lay ahead? Could he live up to the expectations that had always been placed upon him? The thought of living in a government college hostel, sharing a room with strangers, and adjusting to a new environment was overwhelming.

Karan approached him with a drink in hand, a mischievous grin on his face. "Ready for the toast, Arjun?"

Arjun laughed, taking the glass. "As ready as I'll ever be."

Karan clinked his glass against Arjun's, his expression turning serious for a moment. "We're going to miss you, man. But I know you'll do great. NIT is lucky to have you."

"Thanks, Karan. I'll miss you guys too. But hey, it's not like I'm disappearing. I'll be back during the holidays."

They both laughed, and Arjun felt a surge of gratitude for his friends. They had been his constant companions through school, and their support meant the world to him. The thought of being away from them added another layer of anxiety to his departure.

As the party wound down, Arjun found a quiet corner of the garden and sat down, reflecting on the night. The fairy lights cast a warm glow, and he could hear the distant hum of conversations and laughter. He felt a sense of bittersweet nostalgia – a chapter of his life was closing, but a new one was about to begin. His thoughts drifted to the future, imagining the challenges and opportunities that awaited him at NIT. The stories he had heard from seniors about the rigorous academic schedule, the vibrant campus life, and the lifelong friendships that were formed.

Later that night, as he lay in bed staring at the ceiling, Arjun's mind raced with thoughts of the days to come. The sheltered life he had known was about to change drastically. He would have to navigate the academic pressures, the unfamiliar environment, and the inevitable loneliness of being away from home. He wondered what his roommates would be like, whether he would be able to adjust to the mess food, and how he would manage without the comforts he had always taken for granted.

The walls of his room were adorned with posters of his favourite bands, trophies from various school competitions, and photographs capturing cherished memories. Each item held a story, a piece of his life that he was leaving behind. His eyes fell on a framed picture of his family, taken during their last vacation. His mother's radiant smile, his father's proud stance, and his younger sister's playful grin – the image filled him with a sense of warmth and longing. He walked around the room, running his fingers over the items on his desk, feeling a pang of nostalgia. The medals from swimming competitions, the books that had inspired him, and the countless mementos of his childhood. It was all a part of who he was, and leaving it behind was harder than he had anticipated.

But deep down, a spark of determination ignited. This was his chance to step out of the shadows of his parents' protection and become his own person. The journey would be tough, but Arjun was ready to face it head-on. He was eager to prove that he could succeed on his own merits, to show everyone – and himself – that he was more than just a pampered boy. He knew that NIT would be a different world, one that required resilience, hard work, and independence. He felt a mix of fear and excitement at the prospect of discovering who he truly was outside the sheltered environment he had always known.

He turned to his desk, where his bags were packed and ready. Among the textbooks and essentials, he had slipped in a small notebook. It was a journal he planned to keep, a record of his experiences, thoughts, and growth. Writing had always been a way for him to process his emotions, and he knew this journey would be filled with moments worth capturing. He opened the first page and wrote a simple entry: "The journey begins tomorrow. I don't know what lies ahead, but I'm ready to face it." The act of writing those words gave him a sense of calm and purpose.

Tomorrow, he would leave for NIT. The thought filled him with a mix of dread and excitement. He knew the road ahead would be filled with challenges, but it also promised growth, new friendships, and opportunities to learn. As he drifted off to sleep, a sense of resolve settled over him. This was the beginning of a new chapter in his life, one that would shape him into the person he was meant to be. He imagined the campus, with its beautiful lake and tree-lined pathways, and felt a flicker of anticipation.

And with that step, his transformation would begin.

Chapter 1: Stepping Out

Arjun's first morning at NIT was a whirlwind of emotions. The day began with a wake-up call from his mother, who had slipped into his room to ensure he was up on time. As he groggily opened his eyes, the reality of the day ahead hit him. Today, he would leave the comfort and familiarity of his home for the unknown world of NIT.

"Good morning, Son," his mother said softly, brushing his hair back. "It's a big day today. Your breakfast is ready, and your bags are packed."

Arjun nodded, swallowing the lump in his throat. He got dressed slowly, savouring the last moments in his room, surrounded by the comforts he had taken for granted all his life. Downstairs, his family had gathered for a farewell breakfast. The meal was filled with his favourite dishes, but he barely tasted them, his mind already at NIT.

After breakfast, his father helped him load his bags into the car. His mother fussed over him, making sure he had everything he needed. Finally, it was time to leave. With a final round of hugs and well-wishes, Arjun climbed into the car, waving to his family as they grew smaller in the rear-view mirror.

The drive to NIT was long and gave Arjun plenty of time to think. His thoughts drifted from excitement to apprehension and back again. He tried to imagine what his new life would be like – the friends he would make, the challenges he would face. As they neared the campus, his heart began to race.

NIT was a beautiful campus, sprawling over lush green hills with modern buildings interspersed with old, colonial-era structures. A serene lake lay at the heart of the campus, its calm waters reflecting the sky and surrounding trees. As the car drove through the gates, Arjun felt a mix of awe and anxiety. This was going to be his home for the next four years.

They parked near the hostel, and Arjun's father helped him with his bags. The hostel building was imposing, a mix of concrete and glass, bustling with students moving in and out. Arjun's assigned room was on the third floor. He climbed the stairs, his father following with the heavier bags.

The room was small but functional, with two bunk beds, a study table, and a shared cupboard. His roommates, Rajat and Suresh, were already there, unpacking their belongings. They greeted Arjun with friendly smiles, introducing themselves and offering to help him settle in. Arjun felt a bit of his anxiety melt away. These were the people he would be sharing his life with for the foreseeable future, and they seemed welcoming.

After setting up his corner of the room, Arjun's father gave him a quick pep talk. "Remember, Arjun, this is your time to shine. Focus on your studies, make good friends, and don't hesitate to call us if you need anything."

With a final hug, his father left, leaving Arjun standing in the doorway of his new life. The reality of his situation began to sink in. He was on his own now, and it was up to him to make the most of this opportunity.

Classes began the next day, and Arjun was immediately struck by the intensity of the coursework. The professors were knowledgeable and demanding, and the competition among students was fierce. Arjun found himself struggling to keep up with the pace. The subjects were challenging, and the workload was relentless. He spent long hours in the library, poring over textbooks and notes. The pressure to perform well weighed heavily on him. He had always been a top student, but here at NIT, he was just one among many. It was a humbling experience, and Arjun had to push himself harder than ever before.

The hostel life was another adjustment. Sharing a room with other boys was a far cry from the privacy of his own room back home. The bathrooms were communal, and the food in the mess was a stark contrast to his mother's home-cooked meals. Arjun missed the comforts of home, but he knew he had to adapt.

Despite the challenges, Arjun began to form bonds with his roommates. Rajat was from Mumbai, a laid-back guy with a passion for music. Suresh, from Bangalore, was a tech wizard who loved coding. They spent their evenings together, talking about their classes, their homes, and their dreams for the future. These conversations helped Arjun feel less alone and more connected to his new environment.

One evening, after a particularly gruelling day of classes, Rajat suggested they go to a nearby tea stall. "It's a great place to unwind," he said. "We can have some tea and just relax."

Arjun agreed, eager for a break. The tea stall was a small, unassuming place, but it was bustling with students. They ordered tea and settled on a bench outside. As they sipped their tea, Rajat pulled out a pack of cigarettes and offered one to Arjun.

At first, Arjun hesitated. He had never smoked before, but the stress of the day and the desire to fit in pushed him to accept. He took a drag, coughing at the unfamiliar taste. Rajat and Suresh laughed, but it was good-natured, and soon Arjun found himself joining in.

The tea stall became a regular spot for them. After classes, they would head there, sharing stories and unwinding with tea and cigarettes. It became a part of Arjun's routine, a way to cope with the stress of his new life. But as time went on, he began to realize the habit was taking a toll on him. He found it harder to concentrate in class, and his health was suffering.

One night, as he lay in bed, Arjun thought about his future. He had come to NIT to build a better life, to achieve his dreams. He couldn't let a bad habit derail that. The next day, he resolved to quit smoking. It was tough, but with the support of his friends, he managed to break the habit. Instead of heading to the tea stall, they found other ways to relax – playing sports, going for walks around the lake, and exploring the campus.

As the weeks turned into months, Arjun began to find his footing at NIT. The initial shock and homesickness started to fade, replaced by a growing sense of belonging. He was forming friendships, facing challenges head-on, and slowly but surely, adapting to his new environment. The journey was just beginning, but Arjun was ready for whatever came next.

The beauty of the NIT campus played a significant role in Arjun's adaptation. The lush greenery and the serene lake became his sanctuary. He often took long walks around the lake, finding solace in the calm waters and the gentle rustling of leaves. It was during one of these walks that he met Aisha.

Aisha was a second-year student, majoring in computer science. She was sitting on a bench by the lake, sketching in a notebook. Arjun, curious and drawn by her concentration, approached her. "Hi, I'm Arjun. What are you drawing?"

Aisha looked up, surprised but not annoyed. She smiled and showed him her sketch – a beautiful rendition of the lake and its surroundings. "Just capturing the beauty of this place," she said. "It's my way of unwinding after a long day."

Arjun was impressed. "That's amazing. Do you come here often?"

"Whenever I need a break," Aisha replied. "What about you?"

Arjun nodded. "Yeah, I find it really peaceful here. It's a good escape from the stress of classes."

They continued talking, and Arjun felt an immediate connection with Aisha. She was intelligent, creative, and shared his love for nature. They exchanged numbers and promised to meet up again. Over the next few weeks, their friendship grew. They would often meet by the lake, discussing everything from their classes to their dreams and aspirations.

Aisha became a significant part of Arjun's life. Her presence was calming, and her perspective on life was refreshing. She encouraged him to explore his interests outside of academics and helped him see the bigger picture. With her support, Arjun started participating in extracurricular activities. He joined the music club, rediscovering his passion for playing the guitar, and started contributing to the college magazine.

However, life at NIT wasn't without its challenges. The academic pressure remained intense, and Arjun had to work hard to keep up with the coursework. There were times when he felt overwhelmed, but he had built a support system that helped him through the tough times. His roommates, Rajat and Suresh, were always there to lend an ear or offer advice. And Aisha's belief in him gave him the strength to persevere.

One particular evening, Arjun sat in his room, surrounded by textbooks and notes, preparing for a crucial exam. The stress was getting to him, and he felt the familiar urge to step outside for a cigarette. But he reminded himself of his promise to quit. He took a deep breath and texted Aisha instead.

"Feeling overwhelmed. Need a break," he typed.

A few minutes later, his phone buzzed with a reply. "Meet me by the lake. Let's talk."

Arjun smiled, feeling a sense of relief. He packed up his books and headed out. The cool evening breeze greeted him as he walked to the lake. Aisha was already there, sitting on their usual bench. She greeted him with a warm smile and a thermos of hot chocolate.

"Thought you might need this," she said, handing him a cup.

"Thanks, Aisha," Arjun replied, taking a sip. The rich, warm drink was exactly what he needed.

They sat in comfortable silence for a while, watching the sun set over the lake. The sky was painted in hues of orange and pink, and the water reflected the vibrant colours. It was moments like these that made the challenges of NIT worth it.

"How are you holding up?" Aisha asked, breaking the silence.

"It's tough," Arjun admitted. "The workload is intense, and sometimes I feel like I'm drowning. But I'm trying my best."

Aisha nodded, her expression understanding. "You're doing great, Arjun. Remember, it's okay to feel overwhelmed sometimes. Just take it one step at a time."

Her words were reassuring, and Arjun felt a renewed sense of determination. He knew that the road ahead would be difficult, but he also knew that he wasn't alone. He had friends who cared about him, and he was beginning to realize his own strength.

The next morning, Arjun woke up early, feeling more focused and energized. He decided to start his day with a jog around the lake. The fresh air and the rhythmic sound of his footsteps helped clear his mind. As he jogged, he thought about his journey so far – the initial homesickness, the challenges, and the friendships he had formed. He realized how much he had grown since he first arrived at NIT.

In class, Arjun felt more confident. He participated actively, asking questions and engaging in discussions. His professors noticed the change and appreciated his efforts. The support from his friends and his determination to succeed were paying off.

One day, during a particularly challenging project, Arjun's group was struggling to find a solution. They had been working for hours, and frustration was building. Suresh, ever the tech wizard, suggested taking a break and going for a walk.

"Sometimes, a change of scenery can spark new ideas," he said.

The group agreed, and they headed to the lake. As they walked and talked, ideas began to flow. They discussed different approaches, drawing inspiration from their surroundings. By the time they returned to their workspace, they had a clear plan of action.

The project turned out to be a success, and their professor praised their innovative approach. Arjun felt a sense of accomplishment, knowing that he had contributed significantly to the group's success. It was moments like these that reminded him why he was at NIT – to learn, to grow, and to push his limits.

As the semester progressed, Arjun continued to find his balance. He learned to manage his time effectively, balancing academics, extracurricular activities, and social life. He also made a conscious effort to take care of his health, eating well and exercising regularly. The initial struggles seemed like a distant memory, and Arjun was beginning to thrive in his new environment.

One evening, as Arjun sat by the lake with Aisha, he reflected on his journey. "I can't believe how much has changed since I first arrived here," he said.

Aisha smiled, her eyes reflecting the setting sun. "You've come a long way, Arjun. I'm proud of you."

"Thank you," Arjun replied, feeling a surge of gratitude. "I couldn't have done it without you and the others."

"We're all in this together," Aisha said. "And remember, the journey is just as important as the destination."

Her words resonated with Arjun. He realized that while his goal was to succeed academically and build a successful career, the experiences and relationships he was forming along the way were equally valuable. NIT was shaping him into a well-rounded individual, preparing him for the challenges of the real world.

As the semester drew to a close, Arjun felt a sense of pride and accomplishment. He had faced numerous challenges, but he had also experienced significant growth. The journey was far from over, but he was ready for whatever came next.

With a newfound sense of confidence and a supportive network of friends, Arjun looked forward to the future with optimism. He knew that the road ahead would have its ups and downs, but he was prepared to face them head-on. The lessons he had learned and the friendships he had formed at NIT would guide him through the challenges and opportunities that lay ahead.

And so, with each passing day, Arjun continued to embrace his journey at NIT, determined to make the most of every moment and to become the best version of himself.

Chapter 2: The New Environment

Arjun woke up to the sound of his alarm, feeling disoriented. It took him a moment to remember where he was. This wasn't his comfortable bed in Delhi; this was his new reality at NIT. He glanced around the small room he shared with Rajat and Suresh. The room was functional but far from luxurious. He missed the spaciousness and privacy of his bedroom back home.

He dragged himself out of bed and headed to the communal bathroom. This was one of the hardest adjustments for him. Back home, he had his own bathroom, which was always clean and stocked with fresh towels. Here, he had to share with dozens of other boys, and cleanliness was often an afterthought. The bathroom floors were wet and slippery, the sinks often clogged, and the stalls lacked basic amenities. Arjun forced himself to ignore the conditions, reminding himself that this was part of his new life.

Breakfast in the mess hall was another challenge. Arjun had been spoiled by his mother's cooking, and the mess food was a stark contrast. The meals were basic and often repetitive – rice, dal, and a vegetable curry that lacked flavour. The cleanliness of the dining area was also questionable. Flies buzzed around, and the tables were sticky. Arjun found it difficult to eat, his appetite diminished by the surroundings and the quality of the food.

Despite these initial struggles, Arjun knew he had to adapt. He couldn't let these discomforts distract him from his main goal – succeeding at NIT. He started by making small changes. He bought a few supplies to make his room feel more like home – a comfortable pillow, a small fan, and a few posters to decorate the walls. These small touches made a big difference in making the space his own.

He also found ways to cope with the mess food. On weekends, he and his friends would explore the nearby town, discovering small eateries that served delicious, home-cooked meals. These outings became a highlight of his week, a break from the monotony of the mess food and a chance to bond with his friends.

The shared accommodations were another adjustment. Back home, Arjun had his own space and privacy. Here, he had to share every aspect of his life with his roommates. There were no secrets in a hostel room – from study schedules to personal habits, everything was shared. At first, this lack of privacy was overwhelming. Arjun felt exposed and vulnerable, missing the sanctuary of his private room.

Rajat and Suresh, however, were understanding and supportive. They were going through the same adjustments and were willing to make compromises. They set boundaries and respected each other's space and time. This mutual understanding made living together easier. Slowly, Arjun began to appreciate the companionship and support that came with sharing a room. The late-night conversations, shared meals, and collective problem-solving created a sense of camaraderie that he had never experienced before.

One evening, after a particularly tough day of classes, Arjun returned to his room feeling defeated. The coursework was more challenging than he had anticipated, and he was struggling to keep up. Rajat noticed his mood and suggested they go for a walk around the campus.

"Come on, Arjun. Let's take a break. A walk might help clear your mind," Rajat said, grabbing his jacket.

Arjun reluctantly agreed, and they headed out. The campus was beautiful at night, the pathways lit by soft lights and the air filled with the scent of blooming flowers. They walked in silence for a while, taking in the serenity of the surroundings.

After a while, Rajat spoke. "I know it's tough right now, but it will get better. We just need to give ourselves time to adjust."

Arjun nodded, appreciating the support. "I know. It's just hard to believe sometimes. Everything is so different here."

"That's true, but it's also an opportunity to grow," Rajat said. "We're learning to be independent, to deal with challenges. It's not easy, but it's worth it."

Arjun smiled, feeling a bit more hopeful. "Thanks, Rajat. I needed that."

As they continued their walk, Arjun thought about Rajat's words. He realized that his friend was right. This was an opportunity to grow, to learn resilience and adaptability. He just needed to take it one day at a time.

The next morning, Arjun woke up with a renewed sense of determination. He decided to tackle his challenges head-on. He started by creating a study schedule, breaking down his coursework into manageable chunks. He also made a point to stay organized, keeping his notes and assignments in order.

Arjun's new approach began to pay off. He found that by breaking down his tasks, he was able to manage his workload more effectively. He also started attending study groups, where he could collaborate with his classmates and gain different perspectives on the material. This collaborative learning environment helped him grasp difficult concepts and stay motivated.

In addition to academics, Arjun made an effort to engage in extracurricular activities. He joined the music club, where he met students who shared his passion for music. Playing the guitar and jamming with the club members became a great way to unwind and express himself creatively. He also participated in the college magazine, contributing articles and helping with the editorial process. These activities provided a much-needed balance to his rigorous academic schedule and allowed him to explore his interests.

Despite the improvements, there were still days when Arjun felt overwhelmed. One such day, after a particularly gruelling exam, he returned to his room feeling defeated. He slumped onto his bed, staring at the ceiling.

Suresh noticed his friend's mood and sat down beside him. "Rough day?"

Arjun sighed. "You could say that. The exam was brutal. I don't think I did well."

Suresh nodded sympathetically. "Yeah, it was tough. But remember, one bad exam doesn't define you. We're here to learn and grow, and setbacks are part of the process."

Arjun appreciated the reminder. "Thanks, Suresh. It's just hard to keep perspective sometimes."

"I know. But we're in this together. And we have each other's backs," Suresh said, offering a reassuring smile.

Their conversation was interrupted by a knock on the door. It was Aisha, holding a bag of snacks and a mischievous grin. "I heard you guys had a tough exam. Thought you might need a little pick-me-up."

She handed them the bag, which was filled with their favourite snacks. Arjun's spirits lifted instantly. "Aisha, you're a lifesaver."

She laughed. "I know. Now, how about we take a break and watch a movie? We all deserve it."

The three friends settled in for a relaxing evening, the stress of the day melting away. Moments like these reminded Arjun of the importance of friendship and support. They were all navigating the challenges of NIT together, and their shared experiences were creating bonds that would last a lifetime.

As the semester progressed, Arjun continued to adapt to his new environment. He found ways to manage his discomforts and make the most of his situation. The shared accommodations, while initially challenging, became a source of camaraderie and support. The food in the mess, though not gourmet, was a small price to pay for the independence and growth he was experiencing.

Arjun's journey at NIT was far from easy, but it was shaping him into a resilient and adaptable individual. He was learning to embrace the challenges, finding strength in his friendships and discovering his own capabilities. With each passing day, he grew more confident and prepared to face whatever came next.

One weekend, Rajat, Suresh, Aisha, and Arjun decided to explore the town surrounding NIT. They had heard of a small, family-run restaurant that served delicious home-cooked meals. It was a welcome break from the mess food, and they were all excited for the outing.

The restaurant was a cosy place, with simple decor and a warm atmosphere. The owner, an elderly woman, greeted them with a kind smile and recommended some of their specialties. They ordered a variety of dishes, savouring the rich flavours and the feeling of a home-cooked meal.

As they ate, they talked about their experiences at NIT, sharing stories of their struggles and triumphs. The conversation turned to their dreams and aspirations, and Arjun felt a sense of camaraderie and belonging. These friends had become his second family, and their support was helping him navigate the challenges of college life.

After the meal, they decided to explore the local market. The market was bustling with activity, filled with vendors selling everything from fresh produce to handmade crafts. They wandered through the stalls, taking in the sights and sounds. Arjun found himself relaxing and enjoying the experience, feeling more at ease with each passing moment.

Back at the hostel, Arjun reflected on the day. The outing had been a welcome break from the routine, and it had reminded him of the importance of balance. While academics were important, so were friendships and experiences outside of the classroom. He resolved to make time for both, ensuring that he enjoyed his journey at NIT to the fullest.

As the weeks turned into months, Arjun's adaptation to NIT continued. He found a rhythm that worked for him, balancing his studies with extracurricular activities and social time. He continued to participate in the music club, where he formed a band with a few other members. They performed at college events, and the experience was both exhilarating and rewarding.

Arjun also took on more responsibilities with the college magazine, helping to organize events and mentor new members. The sense of purpose and accomplishment he gained from these activities boosted his confidence and helped him feel more integrated into the college community.

One evening, as Arjun and his friends were studying in the library, they received a surprise visit from Nikhil, a senior they had met during their first weeks at NIT. Nikhil had taken a liking to Arjun and his friends, offering guidance and support whenever they needed it.

"Hey guys, how's it going?" Nikhil asked, pulling up a chair.

"We're hanging in there," Rajat replied. "Just trying to survive this semester."

Nikhil chuckled. "I remember those days. It gets better, trust me. You just have to keep pushing through."

Arjun smiled, appreciating Nikhil's words of encouragement. "Thanks, Nikhil. It means a lot coming from you."

"Anytime," Nikhil said. "By the way, there's a cultural fest coming up next month. You guys should definitely participate. It's a great way to take a break from studies and have some fun."

The suggestion piqued their interest. They had heard about the cultural fest but hadn't given it much thought. Now, with Nikhil's encouragement, they decided to sign up for a few events.

The cultural fest turned out to be a highlight of their semester. The campus came alive with music, dance, and art. Students from different departments showcased their talents, and the atmosphere was electric. Arjun's band performed at the fest, and their performance was met with enthusiastic applause. It was a moment of pride and joy, a reminder of the diverse experiences that NIT had to offer.

Participating in the fest also helped Arjun forge new connections. He met students from different disciplines, expanding his social circle and gaining new perspectives. The sense of community and shared enthusiasm further deepened his sense of belonging at NIT.

As the semester drew to a close, Arjun reflected on his journey so far. The initial culture shock of shared accommodations and communal living had given way to a sense of camaraderie and support.

The struggles with food and cleanliness had also become manageable. He had learned to appreciate the small pleasures, like weekend outings and home-cooked meals from local eateries. These experiences added a richness to his life that he hadn't anticipated.

Most importantly, Arjun had discovered his own resilience. He had faced numerous challenges, but he had also grown in ways he couldn't have imagined. The journey was far from over, but he felt more equipped to handle whatever came next.

With the support of his friends and the lessons he had learned, Arjun was ready to continue his journey at NIT. He knew that there would be more challenges ahead, but he also knew that he had the strength and determination to overcome them. And with each passing day, he felt more confident in his ability to thrive in this new environment.

As Arjun prepared for the upcoming semester, a wave of excitement and anticipation washed over him. He was eager to embrace the opportunities and experiences that awaited, knowing that he was on a journey of growth and discovery. NIT was more than just a place for academic learning; it was where he was evolving into the person he was destined to become.

With renewed determination and a strong network of supportive friends, Arjun continued his journey at NIT, ready to tackle the challenges and seize the opportunities ahead. This new environment had become his home, and he was prepared to make the most of it.

Chapter 3: The Academic Pressure

Arjun sat in the lecture hall, his notebook open and pen poised, ready to absorb the first lecture of the semester. The room was filled with eager students, all vying for the top spot in their classes. The energy was palpable, a mix of excitement and anxiety. As the professor walked in, the room fell silent, and Arjun braced himself for what was to come.

Dr. Rao, a distinguished professor of Electrical Engineering, began the lecture with a brief introduction. His reputation preceded him – known for his deep knowledge and rigorous teaching style. "Welcome to Electrical Circuits," he said, his voice commanding attention. "This course will challenge you, but I assure you, it will also be rewarding."

Arjun listened intently, trying to keep up with the rapid pace at which Dr. Rao explained complex concepts. The professor's teaching style was direct and demanding, expecting students to grasp intricate theories quickly. Arjun's initial confidence began to waver as he struggled to understand the material.

After the lecture, Arjun walked out of the hall, feeling overwhelmed. He had always excelled in academics, but this was a different level of intensity. The competitive atmosphere added to the pressure, as students around him discussed the lecture with ease. Arjun realized he needed to step up his game to keep up with the coursework.

The next few weeks were a whirlwind of lectures, assignments, and lab sessions. Each professor had a unique teaching style, adding to the complexity of the courses. Dr. Menon, who taught Advanced Mathematics, was methodical and precise, focusing on problem-solving techniques. Dr. Kapoor, the professor for Digital Electronics, was engaging and interactive, often using real-world examples to explain abstract concepts. While these diverse styles enriched Arjun's learning experience, they also demanded constant adaptation and focus.

Arjun's struggle became evident as the first round of assignments and quizzes approached. The coursework was relentless, with each subject requiring significant time and effort. Arjun found himself buried in textbooks and notes, often studying late into the night. His roommates, Rajat and Suresh, were equally immersed in their studies, and the room often turned into a late-night study hub.

Despite his efforts, Arjun's performance in the initial quizzes was disappointing. He had underestimated the difficulty and overestimated his grasp of the subjects. The realization hit him hard, shaking his confidence. He felt a mix of frustration and self-doubt, questioning his ability to succeed at NIT.

One evening, after receiving a particularly low score on a math quiz, Arjun sat in his room, staring at the paper in disbelief. Rajat noticed his dejection and sat beside him. "Tough quiz, huh?"

Arjun sighed. "I thought I had it figured out, but I barely passed. It's just so much harder than I expected."

Rajat nodded sympathetically. "Yeah, it's a different ball game here. But we can't let one quiz define us. We need to find better ways to study and understand the material."

Arjun appreciated Rajat's perspective. "You're right. I need to change my approach. Maybe join a study group or get some help from the professors."

With renewed determination, Arjun decided to seek help. He approached Dr. Menon after class, explaining his struggles and asking for guidance. Dr. Menon listened patiently, offering practical advice on study techniques and problem-solving strategies. "Focus on understanding the concepts, not just memorizing formulas," he advised. "Practice regularly and don't hesitate to ask questions in class."

Arjun also joined a study group with a few classmates who shared his challenges. They met regularly, discussing difficult topics, solving problems together, and sharing resources. The collaborative learning environment helped Arjun gain new perspectives and clarified many of his doubts.

Balancing the coursework with other commitments was another challenge. Arjun had to manage his time effectively, ensuring he dedicated enough hours to each subject while also participating in extracurricular activities. He created a study schedule, allocating specific time slots for each subject and sticking to it diligently.

Despite the rigorous schedule, Arjun made sure to take breaks and unwind. He continued his evening walks around the lake, finding solace in the serene surroundings. Music remained a significant part of his life, and he often played his guitar to relax. These activities helped him maintain a balance, preventing burnout and keeping him motivated.

The mid-semester exams were a crucial milestone. Arjun's preparation was intense, with long hours spent in the library and study sessions with his group. The exams were challenging, testing not only his knowledge but also his resilience. Arjun approached each paper with a mix of determination and nervousness, knowing that his hard work would pay off.

The results were a pleasant surprise. Arjun's scores had improved significantly, reflecting his efforts and the changes he had made in his study approach. He felt a sense of accomplishment, knowing that he had overcome the initial setbacks and made progress. The experience taught him the value of perseverance and adaptability.

However, the journey was far from over. The academic pressure continued, with new assignments, projects, and presentations adding to the workload. Arjun had to stay on top of his game, constantly pushing himself to excel. He continued to seek help from professors, participate in study groups, and refine his study techniques.

One particular project in Digital Electronics required Arjun to work with a team to design and implement a functional circuit. The project was complex, involving both theoretical knowledge and practical application. Arjun's team consisted of students with diverse skills, and they had to collaborate effectively to succeed.

The initial stages of the project were challenging. There were disagreements on the design approach, and coordinating everyone's efforts was difficult. Arjun, who was naturally introverted, found it hard to assert his ideas and lead the team. The project was at risk of falling behind schedule, and the stress was mounting.

Recognizing the need for effective teamwork, Arjun decided to step out of his comfort zone. He organized a meeting, encouraging open communication and brainstorming. "We all have great ideas, but we need to work together to make this project a success," he said, trying to inspire his teammates.

The meeting proved to be a turning point. The team members began to listen to each other, combining their strengths and compensating for each other's weaknesses. Arjun took on a coordinating role, ensuring tasks were distributed evenly and deadlines were met. The experience taught him valuable lessons in leadership and collaboration.

As the project progressed, Arjun's confidence grew. He was able to contribute meaningfully, applying the theoretical knowledge he had gained in class to practical scenarios. The team's hard work culminated in a successful presentation, earning them high praise from Dr. Kapoor and a top grade.

Arjun's struggles and successes in academics also highlighted the importance of mental health. The constant pressure and high expectations could take a toll, and it was essential to find ways to cope. Arjun made a conscious effort to stay connected with his family, regularly calling his parents and sharing his experiences. Their encouragement and support were a source of strength.

He also leaned on his friends, who were going through similar challenges. They shared their struggles, celebrated their successes, and supported each other through tough times. This sense of community and solidarity was crucial in maintaining a positive mindset.

One evening, after a long day of classes and study sessions, Arjun and his friends gathered in the common room. They were exhausted but decided to unwind with a movie. As they laughed and relaxed, Arjun realized how far he had come. The initial struggles seemed distant, replaced by a sense of belonging and achievement.

The end of the semester brought a mix of relief and reflection. Arjun had faced intense academic pressure, but he had also grown in ways he hadn't anticipated. He had developed effective study strategies, built strong relationships with his professors and peers, and discovered his resilience.

Looking ahead, Arjun knew that the challenges would continue, but he felt more prepared to face them. The journey at NIT was shaping him into a well-rounded individual, equipped with the knowledge and skills to succeed in the competitive world of engineering.

As he prepared for the next semester, Arjun felt a sense of excitement and anticipation. He was ready to embrace the opportunities and experiences that lay ahead, knowing that he was on a path of growth and discovery. The academic pressure at NIT was not just a challenge; it was a catalyst for personal and intellectual development.

With each passing day, Arjun continued to thrive at NIT, determined to make the most of every opportunity and to become the best version of himself. The journey was far from over, but he was ready for whatever came next, confident in his ability to succeed and grow.

The first few months at NIT had been a whirlwind, but as Arjun looked back, he realized how much he had accomplished. The initial sense of being overwhelmed had transformed into a structured routine that included intensive study sessions, collaboration with peers, and occasional breaks to recharge. This balance was critical to his success and well-being.

Arjun also started to develop a closer relationship with his professors. Initially, he had been hesitant to approach them, fearing that his questions might seem trivial. However, he soon realized that the professors appreciated his willingness to learn and were more than willing to help. Dr. Rao, for instance, began to recognize Arjun's determination and provided additional resources and guidance. This mentorship was invaluable, offering Arjun insights that went beyond the textbook.

In one instance, Dr. Menon invited Arjun and a few other students to his office to discuss a particularly challenging topic in Advanced Mathematics. The session was intense but incredibly rewarding. Dr. Menon's approach was to challenge his students to think critically and apply their knowledge in novel ways. This experience not only helped Arjun improve his understanding of the subject but also boosted his confidence.

The study group Arjun had joined also played a significant role in his academic journey. The group consisted of students from various backgrounds, each bringing their unique strengths to the table. Their discussions often extended beyond the coursework, touching on real-world applications and innovative solutions. This collaborative learning environment fostered a deeper understanding of the material and helped Arjun stay motivated.

Despite the rigorous academic schedule, Arjun continued to make time for his extracurricular interests. The music club became a sanctuary where he could express himself creatively and take a break from the academic grind. The club members were supportive, and their shared passion for music created a strong bond. Performing at college events was exhilarating and provided a much-needed outlet for stress.

Arjun also found solace in writing for the college magazine. This allowed him to explore his creative side and connect with students from different disciplines. The editorial meetings were lively and intellectually stimulating, providing a break from the technical rigor of his engineering courses.

As the semester progressed, Arjun began to find a rhythm. He learned to prioritize tasks, manage his time effectively, and seek help when needed. His initial struggles had taught him resilience and adaptability. He also realized the importance of self-care, ensuring he got enough rest and maintained a healthy lifestyle.

One weekend, Arjun and his friends decided to take a short trip to a nearby hill station. The break from the routine was refreshing, and the natural beauty of the hills provided a perfect backdrop for relaxation and reflection. The trip strengthened their bond and reminded them of the importance of taking time to recharge.

Returning to campus, Arjun felt rejuvenated and ready to tackle the remaining challenges of the semester. He approached his studies with renewed vigour, applying the strategies he had learned over the past months. The final exams were intense, but Arjun felt prepared. He had developed a solid understanding of the material and was confident in his abilities.

The end-of-semester results were a testament to his hard work and determination. Arjun had not only passed his courses but had also scored high marks in several subjects. The sense of accomplishment was overwhelming, and he felt a deep sense of gratitude for the support he had received from his friends, professors, and family.

As he looked ahead to the next semester, Arjun felt a sense of optimism. The journey at NIT had been challenging, but it had also been incredibly rewarding. He had grown both academically and personally, developing skills that would serve him well in his future career.

Arjun knew that the road ahead would continue to be demanding, but he was ready. The experiences of the past semester had equipped him with the tools to navigate the challenges that lay ahead. He was determined to make the most of his time at NIT, embracing each opportunity for learning and growth.

With the support of his friends, the guidance of his professors, and his own resilience, Arjun was confident in his ability to succeed. The academic pressure at NIT had been a crucible, forging him into a more capable and determined individual. As he prepared for the next chapter of his journey, Arjun felt a deep sense of purpose and anticipation.

The journey was far from over, but Arjun was ready to face whatever came next. He knew that with hard work, determination, and the support of his community, he could achieve his goals and make a meaningful impact in the world of engineering. And so, with a heart full of hope and a mind ready for the challenges ahead, Arjun continued his journey at NIT, determined to thrive and succeed.

Chapter 4: Making Friends

Arjun stood at the threshold of his dorm room, taking a deep breath. He had always been more comfortable in small, familiar circles, but college demanded that he step out of his comfort zone. Making friends was crucial, not just for companionship but also for support in the challenging academic environment of NIT.

His roommates, Rajat and Suresh, were already seated at the common study table. Rajat was strumming his guitar, a soft melody filling the room, while Suresh was buried in a coding book. They had been friendly and supportive since the beginning, but Arjun knew he needed to expand his social circle beyond just his roommates.

"Hey guys," Arjun started, "I was thinking, we should try to meet more people in the hostel. Maybe invite them over for a jam session or something?"

Rajat looked up from his guitar, a smile spreading across his face. "That's a great idea, Arjun. Music is a great icebreaker. Let's do it this weekend."

Suresh nodded in agreement. "I can help with the planning. Maybe we can put up a notice in the common room and see who's interested."

With the plan set in motion, Arjun felt a mix of excitement and nervousness. He had always found it challenging to initiate conversations and connect with new people, but he knew this was a necessary step. Over the next few days, he and his roommates spread the word about their impromptu jam session, hoping to attract a diverse group of students.

The night of the jam session arrived, and Arjun's room was buzzing with activity. A group of students had gathered, bringing along various instruments and an infectious energy. The atmosphere was lively, with music filling the air and conversations flowing freely.

Arjun found himself in a corner, tuning his guitar and observing the scene. A girl with a bright smile and a confident demeanour approached him. "Hi, I'm Kavya. Heard you guys were hosting this jam session. Mind if I join?"

Arjun smiled, feeling a bit more at ease. "Of course, Kavya. The more, the merrier."

As the night progressed, Arjun noticed how music served as a bridge, connecting people from different backgrounds and disciplines. He played a few of his favourite songs, feeling the tension melt away with each strum of his guitar. Kavya, Rajat, and a few others joined in, creating a harmonious blend of voices and instruments.

By the end of the session, Arjun felt a sense of accomplishment. He had not only enjoyed the evening but had also taken the first step towards forming new friendships. Kavya, Rajat, Suresh, and a few others stayed back, chatting about their interests, classes, and hometowns. These conversations were the foundation of what would become Arjun's first friend group at NIT.

Over the next few weeks, Arjun's new friend group began to take shape. They started meeting regularly, bonding over late-night study sessions, shared meals, and the inevitable hostel shenanigans. Each member of the group brought something unique to the table, enriching their collective experience.

Rajat's love for music often turned their study breaks into mini-concerts. Suresh, with his tech expertise, became the go-to person for any computer-related issues. Kavya's outgoing personality helped keep the group connected and organized. Arjun, though initially reserved, found himself contributing more, especially during group discussions and study sessions.

One evening, the group gathered in the common room for a study session. They had a tough exam coming up, and the pressure was on. Arjun had always been disciplined in his studies, but he found that studying with friends made the process more enjoyable and less stressful. They quizzed each other, shared notes, and explained difficult concepts, turning a daunting task into a collaborative effort.

During a break, Kavya brought out a deck of cards, suggesting a quick game to unwind. The group eagerly agreed, and soon the room was filled with laughter and playful banter. These moments of camaraderie were invaluable, providing a much-needed respite from the academic pressures.

Despite the growing bond, forming and maintaining friendships in a competitive environment wasn't without its challenges. The pressure to perform academically sometimes led to tensions within the group. There were moments of frustration and misunderstandings, especially when the stress levels were high.

One such incident occurred during a particularly stressful week of exams and project deadlines. Rajat, feeling overwhelmed, snapped at Suresh during a study session. "Can you stop fiddling with your laptop and help us with this problem? We're all struggling here!"

Suresh, taken aback, responded defensively. "I am helping, Rajat! Maybe if you paid attention to the discussion instead of strumming your guitar, you'd know that."

The tension in the room was palpable, and Arjun felt a knot forming in his stomach. He had always avoided confrontation, but he knew that ignoring the issue would only make things worse. Summoning his courage, he intervened.

"Guys, let's take a step back," Arjun said, trying to keep his voice calm. "We're all stressed, but arguing won't help. Let's take a short break and come back with a fresh perspective."

The group reluctantly agreed, dispersing to different corners of the room. Arjun felt a mix of relief and anxiety, hoping that the break would help cool things down. After a while, they reconvened, and the atmosphere was noticeably calmer. Rajat apologized to Suresh, and they resumed their study session with renewed focus.

This incident, though stressful, strengthened their bond. They realized the importance of communication and supporting each other, especially during challenging times. The group established a few ground rules to ensure that such conflicts were managed constructively in the future.

Beyond the academic pressures, the group found joy in the small moments of hostel life. Late-night conversations on the hostel terrace, shared meals in the mess, and impromptu trips to the nearby tea stall became cherished rituals. These experiences created a sense of belonging and made the hostel feel like home.

One night, after a particularly intense study session, the group decided to unwind with a game of truth or dare. The game started off light-hearted, with dares involving silly tasks like singing loudly in the corridor or doing a funny dance. However, as the night progressed, the truths revealed deeper aspects of their personalities and experiences.

When it was Arjun's turn, Kavya asked him, "Truth or dare?"

Arjun, feeling adventurous, chose truth. Kavya smiled mischievously and asked, "What's your biggest fear about being here at NIT?"

Arjun hesitated, the question hitting close to home. He took a deep breath and answered honestly. "I guess my biggest fear is not being good enough. I've always been comfortable in my own bubble, and being here, surrounded by so many talented people, makes me doubt myself sometimes."

There was a moment of silence, and then Rajat spoke up. "We all feel that way, Arjun. You're not alone. But look at how far we've come already. We're in this together."

The group nodded in agreement, and Arjun felt a wave of relief. Sharing his insecurities and hearing his friends' support made him feel less alone. It reinforced the idea that their friendship was a source of strength, helping them navigate the ups and downs of college life.

As the semester progressed, the group faced more challenges but also celebrated numerous successes. They supported each other through tough exams, celebrated birthdays with impromptu parties, and tackled projects together. The dynamics within the group evolved, with each member playing a crucial role in their collective journey.

Arjun, who had initially struggled to break out of his shell, found himself becoming more confident and outgoing. He took on leadership roles in group projects, organized study sessions, and even initiated social events. The friendships he had formed were not only helping him academically but also contributing to his personal growth.

One weekend, the group decided to take a break from their studies and go on a hike to a nearby hill. The hike was challenging but rewarding, with breathtaking views and the joy of reaching the summit together. They spent the day exploring, taking pictures, and enjoying each other's company. The experience further strengthened their bond and created lasting memories.

Back at the hostel, they gathered in Arjun's room, exhausted but happy. Kavya suggested they start a tradition of weekend outings, exploring different places around the campus. The group eagerly agreed, excited about the prospect of new adventures.

As the semester drew to a close, Arjun reflected on his journey. The initial challenge of breaking out of his shell and making friends had transformed into one of the most rewarding aspects of his college experience. The friendships he had formed were a source of support, joy, and growth, helping him navigate the complexities of NIT.

Looking ahead, Arjun felt a sense of gratitude and optimism. He knew that the road ahead would have its challenges, but he was confident in his ability to face them with the support of his friends. The journey at NIT was not just about academics; it was about the relationships and experiences that were shaping him into a well-rounded individual.

As Arjun settled into his new life at NIT, the bonds within his friend group deepened. The shared experiences and the support they provided each other were instrumental in helping him navigate the various challenges that came their way. The group's dynamics were ever-evolving, with each member contributing to the collective strength.

One evening, after a long day of classes, Arjun and his friends decided to explore the town just outside the campus. It was a bustling place with narrow streets lined with shops, eateries, and vendors selling everything from fresh produce to handmade crafts. The group wandered through the market, sampling local snacks and enjoying the vibrant atmosphere.

They stumbled upon a quaint café tucked away in a corner, its warm lights and inviting aroma drawing them in. The café quickly became their favourite hangout spot, a place where they could unwind, chat, and enjoy good food. These outings became a regular affair, adding a new dimension to their friendship.

Back on campus, the group continued to support each other academically. They formed study groups for different subjects, leveraging each other's strengths to tackle difficult concepts. Kavya, who was particularly good at Mathematics, helped the others with their calculus problems. Rajat, with his knack for electronics, guided them through the intricacies of circuit design. Suresh, ever the tech wizard, simplified complex programming assignments for the group.

Arjun found his niche in organizing and coordinating these study sessions. His methodical approach ensured that they covered all necessary topics while keeping the sessions engaging and interactive. The collective effort paid off, with the group consistently performing well in their exams and assignments.

However, the journey wasn't always smooth. The pressure of maintaining good grades, combined with the personal challenges each member faced, sometimes led to conflicts. One such instance occurred during the preparation for a major project presentation. The group had divided the tasks among themselves, but Kavya, overwhelmed by her commitments, was falling behind.

Rajat, frustrated by the delay, confronted her during a study session. "Kavya, we need your part of the project done. We're running out of time!"

Kavya, visibly stressed, snapped back. "I know, Rajat! I'm doing my best. But I have other responsibilities too."

The tension was thick, and Arjun knew he had to intervene. "Guys, let's not turn this into a blame game. Kavya, we understand you're under a lot of pressure. How can we help you catch up?"

Kavya, her anger subsiding, took a deep breath. "I could use some help with the research. If someone could assist me, I can focus on compiling the data."

Suresh immediately volunteered. "I'll help you with the research. We can meet after dinner and work on it together."

The crisis was averted, and the group managed to complete the project on time. The experience reinforced the importance of communication and collaboration. They learned to be more empathetic towards each other's struggles and to offer help without judgment.

In addition to their academic pursuits, the group participated in various extracurricular activities. They joined clubs, attended workshops, and volunteered for events. These activities not only enriched their college experience but also provided opportunities to meet new people and expand their social network.

Arjun, who had initially been hesitant to step out of his comfort zone, found himself thriving in these new environments. He discovered a passion for event management and started taking on leadership roles in organizing college festivals and cultural events. The skills he developed through these experiences were invaluable, boosting his confidence and broadening his horizons.

One memorable event was the annual cultural festival, a grand affair that brought together students from different departments to showcase their talents. Arjun, along with his friends, played a significant role in organizing the event. They spent weeks planning, coordinating, and rehearsing for the various performances.

The festival was a resounding success, with students showcasing their skills in music, dance, drama, and more. Arjun's band performed to an enthusiastic crowd, their music resonating with the audience. The sense of accomplishment and the joy of creating something meaningful with his friends was a highlight of his college journey.

As the festival drew to a close, the group gathered on the terrace of the hostel, reflecting on their journey so far. The night sky was clear, and the stars seemed to shine brighter, mirroring the sense of fulfilment they all felt.

"Can you believe how far we've come?" Kavya said, her voice filled with wonder. "From strangers to friends, and now, we're organizing festivals and acing exams together."

Rajat nodded, strumming his guitar softly. "Yeah, it's been an incredible journey. And the best part is, we did it together."

Arjun smiled, feeling a deep sense of gratitude. "I couldn't have asked for a better group of friends. You guys have made this experience unforgettable."

Suresh, always the practical one, added, "And we've got a long way to go. More challenges, more adventures. But as long as we stick together, we can handle anything."

The group sat in comfortable silence, the bonds of friendship stronger than ever. They knew that the road ahead would have its ups and downs, but they were ready to face it together. The experiences they had shared and the support they provided each other were the foundation of their strength.

As the semester drew to a close, Arjun reflected on his journey. The initial challenge of breaking out of his shell and making friends had transformed into one of the most rewarding aspects of his college experience. The friendships he had formed were a source of support, joy, and growth, helping him navigate the complexities of NIT.

Looking ahead, Arjun felt a sense of gratitude and optimism. He knew that the road ahead would have its challenges, but he was confident in his ability to face them with the support of his friends. The journey at NIT was not just about academics; it was about the relationships and experiences that were shaping him into a well-rounded individual.

With a heart full of hope and a mind ready for the challenges ahead, Arjun continued his journey at NIT, determined to thrive and succeed. The friendships he had formed were a testament to the power of stepping out of his comfort zone, embracing new experiences, and finding joy in the journey. The lessons learned and the bonds created would stay with him, guiding him through the rest of his college years and beyond.

And so, with the support of his friends and the strength he had discovered within himself, Arjun faced the future with confidence and determination. The journey was far from over, but he was ready for whatever came next, knowing that he was not alone. The friendships he had made at NIT were not just a part of his college life; they were a part of him, shaping his identity and enriching his soul.

Chapter 5: Ragging and Bonding

It was nearing midnight, and Arjun was sitting on his bed, flipping through his notes, trying to focus on his studies. The hostel was unusually quiet, the usual chatter and noise replaced by a tense silence. He had heard whispers about the infamous ragging sessions conducted by the seniors, and his stomach churned at the thought. He had managed to avoid any direct encounters so far, but tonight felt different.

Just as he tried to push the thought out of his mind, his phone buzzed. It was a message from Nikhil, a senior known for his stern demeanour. The message was short and to the point: "12 am. Senior hostel. Room 307. Don't be late."

Arjun's heart raced. He glanced at Rajat and Suresh, who had received similar messages. The anxiety in the room was palpable. A few others joined them, all wearing the same apprehensive expressions.

"What do we do?" Rajat asked, her voice trembling slightly.

"We don't have much of a choice," Suresh replied. "We have to go. If we don't, it will only make things worse."

Arjun nodded, trying to steady his nerves. "Let's stick together and get through this."

As the clock struck midnight, they made their way to the senior hostel. The corridors were dimly lit, and the air was thick with tension. They arrived at Room 307, hesitating for a moment before knocking on the door.

Nikhil opened the door, flanked by Archit, Akshay, and Prateek. The seniors' faces were stern, their eyes assessing the group of juniors standing before them.

"Welcome," Nikhil said, his voice dripping with authority. "We've been expecting you."

The group was ushered into the room, where they were instructed to kneel on the floor. The next four hours were gruelling. The seniors commanded them to perform various humiliating tasks – dancing, singing, and answering absurd questions. Each task was met with laughter and taunts from the seniors, testing the juniors' patience and resilience.

Arjun struggled to keep his composure. The physical discomfort was one thing, but the emotional strain of being mocked and humiliated was harder to bear. He glanced at his friends, seeing the same determination in their eyes. They were in this together, and that thought gave him strength.

At one point, Arjun, feeling the tension getting the better of him, couldn't help but laugh at the absurdity of the situation. The seniors, initially taken aback, soon focused their attention on him.

"You think this is funny?" Akshay snapped. "Let's see you dance then, Mr. Comedian."

Arjun felt a surge of fear but forced himself to stand up. He began to dance awkwardly, his movements stiff and uncomfortable. The room erupted in laughter, the seniors jeering and mocking him. But as the minutes passed, Arjun found himself relaxing slightly, his fear giving way to a strange sense of defiance. He realized that by laughing and dancing, he was taking away some of the power the seniors held over him.

The session continued, each task pushing the juniors to their limits. But amidst the humiliation and exhaustion, something unexpected happened. The seniors began to ease up, their taunts turning into casual banter. The atmosphere in the room shifted subtly, the tension slowly dissipating.

After what felt like an eternity, Nikhil called the session to an end. "Alright, that's enough for tonight," he said, his tone less severe. "You guys can go."

Arjun and his friends stood up, their bodies aching and minds exhausted. But as they made their way out of the room, Nikhil's voice stopped them.

"Wait a minute," he said. "You all did well tonight. Welcome to NIT."

There was a moment of stunned silence before Archit added, "Remember, this was just a test. We all went through it. It's a rite of passage. From now on, if you need anything, you can come to us."

The juniors exchanged surprised glances. The seniors' words felt genuine, a stark contrast to their behaviour over the past four hours. Arjun felt a sense of relief and a flicker of something else – respect.

As they walked back to their hostel, the group was quiet, each lost in their thoughts. They had endured a challenging ordeal, but it had also brought them closer together. The shared experience had forged a bond, not just among themselves but also with the seniors.

The next day, as Arjun went about his classes, he noticed a subtle shift in how the seniors interacted with him and his friends. There was a nod of acknowledgment from Nikhil in the corridor, a friendly pat on the back from Akshay in the mess hall. The ragging session, as gruelling as it was, had earned them a place in the unwritten hierarchy of hostel life.

The camaraderie extended beyond the occasional friendly gesture. The seniors began to offer guidance and support, sharing their own experiences and tips for navigating the challenges of NIT. Nikhil, in particular, took Arjun under his wing, helping him with difficult coursework and offering advice on balancing academics with extracurricular activities.

One evening, as Arjun and his friends were studying in their room, Nikhil dropped by unexpectedly. "Mind if I join you guys?" he asked, a rare smile on his face.

"Sure, come in," Rajat replied, surprised but welcoming.

Nikhil sat down, pulling out his notes. "I heard you guys have a tough exam coming up. Thought I could help."

The study session turned into an informal mentorship, with Nikhil sharing valuable insights and breaking down complex concepts. Arjun was struck by the transformation – the same senior who had tormented them just a few nights ago was now a mentor and ally.

As the weeks went by, the bond with the seniors grew stronger. Archit, Akshay, and Prateek also warmed up to the juniors, often joining them for meals and study sessions. The initial fear and resentment gave way to mutual respect and camaraderie. The ragging session, which had seemed like a nightmarish ordeal, now felt like a rite of passage that had paved the way for meaningful relationships.

One night, Arjun and his friends decided to organize a small gathering to thank the seniors for their support. They pooled their resources, bought snacks, and set up a makeshift party in the common room. The seniors were touched by the gesture, and the evening turned into a celebration of their newfound friendships.

As they sat together, sharing stories and laughter, Nikhil raised a toast. "To new beginnings and lasting friendships," he said, his voice filled with warmth.

Arjun looked around the room, feeling a deep sense of gratitude. The journey at NIT had been challenging, but it was also shaping him in ways he hadn't anticipated. The friendships he had formed, both with his peers and the seniors, were a testament to the power of resilience and camaraderie.

The ragging session had been a trial by fire, but it had also been a catalyst for growth and bonding. Arjun realized that every challenge he faced was an opportunity to learn and connect with others. The experience had taught him the importance of perseverance, empathy, and the strength that comes from standing together.

As the semester progressed, Arjun continued to thrive academically and socially. The support from his friends and the mentorship from the seniors provided a strong foundation for his journey at NIT. He felt more confident and prepared to face the challenges ahead, knowing that he was not alone.

With each passing day, Arjun's bond with his friends and the seniors deepened. They became a close-knit community, supporting each other through thick and thin. The journey at NIT was far from over, but Arjun felt ready to embrace whatever came next, confident in his ability to succeed and grow.

The weeks following the ragging session saw a significant transformation in Arjun's experience at NIT. The fear and apprehension that had marked his initial days began to dissipate, replaced by a sense of belonging and camaraderie. The seniors, who had once been figures of intimidation, were now mentors and friends.

Arjun found himself often in the company of Nikhil, Archit, Akshay, and Prateek. The seniors took an active interest in the juniors' lives, offering advice on everything from study techniques to managing stress. Arjun appreciated their guidance, recognizing that it stemmed from their own experiences of navigating the challenges of NIT.

One evening, after a particularly gruelling day of classes, Nikhil invited Arjun and his friends to join him for tea at a small, inconspicuous stall just outside the campus. It was a place known only to a few, offering a quiet refuge from the hustle and bustle of college life.

The tea stall was run by an elderly man, fondly known as "Chacha" by the students. He greeted Nikhil with a warm smile and quickly prepared their favourite brew. The group settled down on the makeshift benches, the evening air filled with the aroma of freshly brewed tea and the hum of quiet conversation.

"How are you guys holding up?" Nikhil asked, taking a sip of his tea.

Arjun sighed, feeling the weight of the day lifting slightly. "It's been tough, but we're managing. The coursework is intense, but we're getting the hang of it."

Akshay nodded. "It takes time, but you'll find your rhythm. Just remember to take breaks and not let the stress get to you."

Archit chimed in, "And don't hesitate to ask for help. We're all in this together."

The tea sessions became a regular affair, offering a much-needed break from the rigors of academic life. They were a time for casual conversations, shared laughs, and bonding over the simple pleasures of life. The seniors shared stories of their own struggles and triumphs, providing valuable insights and a sense of perspective.

Arjun began to see the seniors not just as mentors but as friends who genuinely cared about their well-being. The hierarchical divide that had initially seemed so daunting now felt more like a bridge, connecting them through shared experiences and mutual respect.

As the semester progressed, the juniors found themselves leaning on the seniors for support in various ways. Nikhil, with his sharp analytical skills, helped Arjun and his friends navigate complex problem sets. Archit, known for his organizational prowess, guided them in managing their time effectively. Akshay and Prateek, with their easy-going nature, provided emotional support, often lightening the mood with their humour and camaraderie.

The transformation in their relationship was most evident during a particularly challenging project. The juniors were tasked with designing a complex circuit, a project that required both theoretical knowledge and practical application. The pressure was immense, and the group often found themselves working late into the night.

One evening, as they were struggling with a particularly stubborn component, Nikhil and Akshay dropped by their room. "Need some help?" Nikhil asked, his tone casual but supportive.

Arjun nodded, feeling a mix of relief and gratitude. "We're stuck with this part. We can't seem to get it right."

Nikhil and Akshay spent the next few hours with them, guiding them through the process, troubleshooting issues, and offering practical solutions. The room was filled with a sense of purpose and collaboration, the stress of the project overshadowed by the support and camaraderie.

By the time they finished, it was well past midnight. The circuit was finally complete, and the group felt a profound sense of accomplishment. Nikhil clapped Arjun on the back, a proud smile on his face. "Well done, guys. You nailed it."

The experience was a turning point for Arjun. It reinforced the importance of teamwork and the value of having a strong support network. The seniors' willingness to help, despite their own busy schedules, was a testament to the bonds they had formed.

Beyond the academic sphere, the bond with the seniors extended to various aspects of hostel life. They often joined the juniors for meals, their presence turning the mundane mess hall into a place of lively conversations and shared laughter. The seniors shared tips on coping with homesickness, managing finances, and balancing academics with extracurricular activities.

One evening, after a particularly stressful week of exams, the seniors organized a surprise outing to a nearby hill station. The trip was a welcome break, offering a chance to relax and rejuvenate. The group spent the day hiking, exploring the scenic beauty, and enjoying each other's company. The outing was filled with moments of joy and camaraderie, strengthening their bonds and creating lasting memories.

As the semester drew to a close, Arjun reflected on the journey so far. The initial fear and apprehension had given way to a sense of belonging and confidence. The ragging session, which had once seemed like a nightmarish ordeal, now felt like a rite of passage that had paved the way for meaningful relationships and personal growth.

The friendships he had formed with the seniors were a source of strength and inspiration. They had taught him valuable lessons in resilience, empathy, and the importance of supporting each other. Arjun felt a deep sense of gratitude for their guidance and support, knowing that they had played a crucial role in shaping his experience at NIT.

Looking ahead, Arjun felt a renewed sense of determination and optimism. He knew that the road ahead would have its challenges, but he was confident in his ability to face them with the support of his friends and mentors. The journey at NIT was not just about academics; it was about the relationships and experiences that were shaping him into a well-rounded individual.

And so, with the support of his friends and the lessons learned from the ragging session, Arjun faced the future with a renewed sense of determination. The journey was challenging, but it was also filled with opportunities for growth and connection. The friendships he had formed were not just a part of his college life; they were a part of his identity, shaping him into the person he was meant to be.

Chapter 6: Extracurricular Activities

Arjun sat in the bustling common room, the noticeboard covered with flyers for various clubs and societies. It was the beginning of his second year at NIT, and he was determined to make the most of his college experience. His first year had been a whirlwind of adjusting to the academic pressures and building friendships, but now he wanted to explore beyond the classroom.

He noticed a flyer for the Film and Music Society, and his interest was piqued. Music had always been a passion, and he saw this as an opportunity to connect with like-minded individuals. He decided to attend the next meeting, curious about what it would entail.

The meeting was lively, with students discussing upcoming events and performances. The enthusiasm was infectious, and Arjun found himself volunteering for the next cultural festival. He was assigned the role of a volunteer coordinator, responsible for managing a team and ensuring that the event ran smoothly.

The experience was both challenging and rewarding. Arjun had to balance his academic responsibilities with the demands of organizing the festival, but he thrived on the excitement and energy. He discovered a knack for leadership, effectively coordinating his team and handling unexpected issues with composure.

The festival was a success, and Arjun's efforts did not go unnoticed. His dedication and organizational skills impressed the senior members, and he was soon promoted to the role of core coordinator for the Film and Music Society. In this role, he had more responsibilities, from planning events to managing budgets and liaising with other clubs.

Arjun's involvement in the Film and Music Society became a significant part of his college life. He organized numerous events, from film screenings and music concerts to talent shows and workshops. His leadership skills continued to grow, and he enjoyed the creative outlet that the society provided.

By his third year, Arjun had become the secretary of the Film and Music Society. This role came with even greater responsibilities but also more opportunities to make an impact. He successfully pulled off several large-scale events, including a week-long cultural festival that featured performances, competitions, and guest lectures by industry professionals.

One of the most memorable events was a music concert that Arjun organized, featuring a popular band. The logistics were complex, from arranging the stage and sound equipment to managing the crowd and ensuring security. The event was a resounding success, attracting a large audience and earning Arjun accolades for his impeccable coordination.

Beyond the Film and Music Society, Arjun's interests extended to his academic field. He decided to found a club dedicated to Electrical Engineering, aiming to create a platform for students to collaborate, share knowledge, and work on innovative projects. The club, named "Electro Innovators," quickly gained traction, attracting students passionate about electronics and technology.

One of the club's first projects was to design and build a smart home automation system. Arjun led the team, guiding them through the research, design, and implementation phases. The project was a huge success, demonstrating the practical applications of their theoretical knowledge and earning recognition from the faculty.

The success of Electro Innovators opened up more opportunities for collaboration and learning. The club organized workshops, guest lectures, and technical competitions, fostering a community of enthusiastic learners. Arjun took great pride in seeing the club grow and evolve, knowing that it was making a meaningful impact on the students' academic and professional development.

In addition to his involvement in clubs and societies, Arjun was also an avid sports enthusiast. He participated in cricket and badminton, enjoying the physical activity and the camaraderie that came with being part of a team. Sports provided a much-needed balance to his hectic schedule, offering a way to unwind and stay fit.

Arjun's dedication to sports was evident in his commitment to practice and his performance in inter-college tournaments. He was a key player in the cricket team, known for his strategic thinking and teamwork. In badminton, he competed in singles and doubles matches, consistently performing well and bringing home several medals.

Balancing academics, extracurricular activities, and sports was not easy, but Arjun managed it with determination and effective time management. He developed a structured schedule, prioritizing tasks and making sure to allocate time for each of his commitments. His ability to juggle multiple responsibilities earned him respect from his peers and professors alike.

The experiences and skills Arjun gained through his extracurricular activities were invaluable. He learned the importance of teamwork, leadership, and communication, all of which contributed to his personal growth and development. These activities also enhanced his resume, showcasing a well-rounded profile that would be attractive to future employers.

As Arjun approached the final year of his degree, he reflected on the journey so far. The decision to actively participate in extracurricular activities had been one of the best choices he had made. It had enriched his college experience, provided opportunities for personal growth, and helped him build a strong network of friends and mentors.

One of the highlights of his final year was organizing the annual technical festival, TechFusion. As the lead coordinator, Arjun had the responsibility of overseeing the entire event, from planning and promotion to execution and evaluation. The festival featured a range of activities, including technical workshops, hackathons, paper presentations, and robotics competitions.

TechFusion was a massive undertaking, requiring meticulous planning and coordination. Arjun assembled a dedicated team, delegating tasks and ensuring that every aspect of the festival was covered. He worked closely with faculty advisors, sponsors, and external partners, building relationships and securing the necessary resources.

The festival was a resounding success, attracting participants from various colleges and showcasing the talent and innovation of NIT students. Arjun's leadership and organizational skills were widely praised, and the experience further solidified his reputation as a capable and dependable leader.

In addition to TechFusion, Arjun continued his involvement with the Film and Music Society, organizing a grand farewell concert for the graduating batch. The concert was a fitting tribute to the seniors, filled with music, dance, and heartfelt speeches. Arjun took the stage to thank his friends and mentors, expressing his gratitude for the incredible journey they had shared.

As his time at NIT drew to a close, Arjun felt a deep sense of fulfilment. The experiences and achievements of the past few years had shaped him into a confident, capable, and well-rounded individual. He had grown not only academically but also personally, developing skills and relationships that would last a lifetime.

Arjun's involvement in extracurricular activities had been a key factor in his personal growth and success. It had taught him the value of hard work, perseverance, and collaboration, and had provided countless opportunities for learning and development. As he prepared to graduate and embark on the next chapter of his life, Arjun felt well-equipped to face the challenges and opportunities that lay ahead.

With immense gratitude and a readiness for new adventures, Arjun eagerly anticipated the future. His time at NIT had been a remarkable journey, rich with joy, learning, and personal growth. The friendships he had forged, the skills he had developed, and the cherished memories he had created would serve as a guiding light throughout his life and career.

Arjun was aware that the future would bring its own set of challenges, but he felt well-prepared to tackle them with determination and resilience. The experiences at NIT had equipped him with the tools to seize new opportunities and make a meaningful impact. Supported by his friends, mentors, and the valuable lessons he had learned, Arjun was ready to step confidently into the future and leave a lasting mark on the world.

Chapter 7: One-Sided Love

Arjun Mehra had always been a dreamer. Even amidst the rigorous demands of NIT, he harboured romantic notions shaped by books, movies, and music. From the first year, he knew of Anuska, a fellow student with a radiant smile and an infectious laugh. However, he never paid much attention to her. She often sought his help in the computer lab, and over time, they began to chat more frequently.

Anuska had a crush on Arjun, and her friend Suresh constantly nudged him to pay attention to her. Initially dismissive, Arjun gradually began to notice her more. Their chats turned into late-night conversations about everything under the sun – from their favorite bands to their deepest fears. As they spent more time together, Arjun felt an emotional bond forming, but he remained unaware of Anuska's feelings for him.

One evening, as they sat by the tranquil campus lake, Anuska shared a personal story about her childhood. Arjun listened intently, captivated by her openness and vulnerability. The moonlight danced on the water's surface, creating a serene backdrop for their conversation. In that moment, Arjun realized he was falling in love.

Encouraged by the depth of their conversations and Anuska's apparent interest in him, Arjun decided to express his feelings. He planned a special evening, inviting Anuska to a quiet spot on campus where they often hung out. He set up a small picnic with her favourite snacks and music, hoping to create a memorable moment.

As they sat together under the starlit sky, Arjun's heart raced. He took a deep breath and said, "Anuska, I've really enjoyed getting to know you these past few months. You mean a lot to me, and I think I'm falling for you."

Anuska's eyes widened in surprise, and for a moment, there was silence. She sighed softly, her expression turning somber. "Arjun, you're one of my closest friends, and I cherish our time together. But there's something you need to know."

Arjun felt his heart sink as Anuska continued, "There's someone else. I've been in love with a senior named Rahul for a while now. I didn't know how to tell you because I didn't want to hurt you."

The words hit Arjun like a punch to the gut. He felt a wave of disappointment and heartache wash over him. "I see," he said quietly, trying to keep his voice steady. "I didn't realize. I just thought... maybe..."

Anuska reached out to hold his hand. "I'm so sorry, Arjun. I never meant to lead you on. You're an amazing person, and you deserve someone who feels the same way about you."

Arjun forced a smile, though his heart ached. "It's okay, Anuska. I appreciate your honesty. I'm glad we talked about this."

The days that followed were difficult for Arjun. The pain of unrequited love was a heavy burden to bear, and he struggled to focus on his studies and extracurricular activities. Nights were the hardest. Arjun would lie in bed, staring at the ceiling, feeling a crushing emptiness. The memories of their conversations and the dreams he had built around her presence haunted him. He often found himself crying into his pillow, the pain too overwhelming to contain.

During the days, Arjun tried to put on a brave face. He immersed himself in his academic responsibilities and leadership roles, but his thoughts constantly wandered back to Anuska. Avoiding her and Rahul became a coping mechanism. He changed his usual routes around campus, skipped group gatherings, and even sat at the back of the class to avoid seeing them together. Each encounter felt like a dagger to his heart, a painful reminder of his unfulfilled dreams. The sight of them laughing together, sharing private jokes, and displaying their affection was too much for him to bear.

Arjun's friends noticed his withdrawal and did their best to support him. They tried to cheer him up with late-night chats, movie nights, and impromptu outings. One evening, as Arjun sat in the common room, lost in thought, his friend Rajat approached him.

"Hey, Arjun, you okay?" Rajat asked, concern evident in his voice.

Arjun sighed deeply. "It's been tough, Rajat. I thought Anuska felt the same way about me, but she loves someone else."

Rajat nodded sympathetically. "I get it, man. Unrequited love can be brutal. But you can't let it define you. You're a strong person, and you'll get through this."

Arjun appreciated Rajat's words, but the journey to healing was a gradual process. He continued to invest his energy in his passions, finding a sense of purpose and fulfillment in his work. Slowly but surely, the pain began to subside, and he felt himself growing stronger.

As time passed, Arjun realized that his experience with Anuska had taught him valuable lessons about love and resilience. He learned the importance of self-worth and the necessity of letting go when things didn't work out as hoped. He also discovered the strength to remain open-hearted, knowing that true love would come in its own time.

The emotional struggle had ultimately led to personal growth, and Arjun emerged from the experience with a newfound sense of clarity and determination. He understood that love was a journey, often fraught with challenges, but also filled with opportunities for growth and self-discovery.

One afternoon, a few months later, Arjun was sitting under a tree on campus, studying for an upcoming exam. He looked up to see Anuska walking towards him, her face lit up with a warm smile. His heart skipped a beat, but he reminded himself of the distance he had put between them.

"Hey, Arjun," Anuska greeted him, sitting down beside him. "I haven't seen you around much lately. How have you been?"

Arjun took a deep breath, steadying himself. "I've been busy with classes and projects. How about you?"

Anuska nodded, her smile faltering slightly. "Same here. I just wanted to say that I miss our conversations. I hope we can still be friends."

Arjun felt a pang of sadness but also a sense of relief. He realized that he had grown enough to handle this conversation without falling apart. "I miss our talks too, Anuska. We can definitely still be friends."

Their friendship continued, albeit with a new dynamic. Arjun learned to appreciate Anuska's presence without harbouring romantic feelings. He focused on his own growth and happiness, knowing that he had emerged stronger from the experience.

In the months that followed, Arjun continued to thrive at NIT. He maintained a strong focus on his academics and extracurricular activities, excelling in his leadership roles and building meaningful connections with his peers. His experience with one-sided love had made him more empathetic and understanding, qualities that further endeared him to his friends and colleagues.

Arjun's story of unrequited love became a poignant chapter in his life, one that shaped him into a more resilient and self-aware individual. He carried the lessons he had learned with him, knowing that they would guide him in future relationships and endeavours.

As Arjun's journey at NIT progressed, his experience with Anuska served as a foundation for his personal growth. He had learned to navigate the complexities of love and heartbreak, emerging stronger and more self-assured. This strengthened resilience later proved invaluable in his new relationship, helping him navigate fresh challenges and strike a balance between his commitments and the demands of love.

Arjun's time at NIT was a testament to his ability to adapt and grow in the face of adversity. The lessons he had learned about love, resilience, and self-worth would continue to shape his journey, guiding him towards a future filled with possibilities and opportunities for growth.

Chapter 8: Love's Second Chance

Arjun Mehra had come a long way since his heartache with Anuska. The pain of unrequited love had shaped him into a more resilient and self-aware individual. As he entered his third year at NIT, he felt ready to open his heart again. He had learned to balance his academic commitments, extracurricular activities, and personal growth, and now he hoped to find a relationship that would complement his journey.

It was during one of the Film and Music Society events that Arjun met Maya. She was a vivacious, confident girl with a keen interest in photography and an infectious enthusiasm for life. Maya had a modern, down-to-earth charm that drew people towards her. Arjun was immediately captivated by her charisma and found himself wanting to know her better.

Their initial interactions were casual and friendly, often revolving around shared interests and group activities. However, as they spent more time together, Arjun felt a deeper connection forming. Late-night chats became a regular part of their routine, where they discussed their dreams, fears, and everything in between.

One evening, as they were walking back to the hostel after a society meeting, Maya turned to Arjun and said, "You know, Arjun, I feel like I can talk to you about anything. You're a great listener."

Arjun smiled, feeling a warmth spread through his chest. "I feel the same way, Maya. You make everything seem brighter and more exciting."

Their friendship gradually deepened, and Arjun found himself falling for Maya. He admired her independence, her passion for photography, and her ability to find joy in the little things. Maya, too, seemed to enjoy Arjun's company, often seeking him out for advice and support.

Encouraged by their growing closeness, Arjun decided to express his feelings. He planned a special evening, inviting Maya to a quiet spot on campus where they often hung out. He set up a small picnic with her favourite snacks and music, hoping to create a memorable moment.

As they sat together under the starlit sky, Arjun's heart raced. He took a deep breath and said, "Maya, I've really enjoyed getting to know you these past few months. You mean a lot to me, and I think I'm falling for you."

Maya's eyes sparkled with surprise and delight. She smiled and took his hand. "Arjun, I've been feeling the same way. I was just waiting for the right moment to tell you."

Relief and joy washed over Arjun as they shared their first kiss. Their relationship blossomed quickly, filled with laughter, shared experiences, and deep conversations. Arjun felt a sense of fulfilment he had never experienced before, and he was determined to make the relationship work.

However, as the semester progressed, balancing his time between studies, friends, and his relationship with Maya became increasingly challenging. Arjun's coursework and extracurricular commitments demanded a lot of his time, and he often found himself struggling to allocate enough time for Maya.

The first signs of strain appeared when Maya mentioned feeling neglected. "Arjun, we hardly spend any quality time together anymore," she said one evening after a particularly hectic week. "I feel like I'm always competing with your studies and your clubs."

Arjun felt a pang of guilt. He cared deeply for Maya and didn't want her to feel side-lined. "I'm sorry, Maya," he said, taking her hand. "I promise I'll make more time for us. It's just been really busy lately."

Despite his best intentions, finding a balance proved challenging. The pressure of upcoming exams and the responsibilities of leading multiple clubs left Arjun with little time to relax, let alone nurture his relationship. He started missing out on spontaneous outings and date nights, opting instead to stay back and work on assignments or prepare for events.

The situation reached a breaking point during the preparation for TechFusion, the annual technical festival. Arjun was deeply involved in organizing the event, often staying up late into the night to ensure everything was on track. Maya, on the other hand, felt increasingly isolated and frustrated.

One evening, after Arjun had cancelled yet another date to attend a meeting, Maya confronted him. "Arjun, this isn't working. I feel like I'm always your last priority. I understand that you're busy, but I need to know that I matter too."

Arjun sighed, feeling the weight of her words. "Maya, I care about you a lot. But this festival is important, and I have responsibilities that I can't ignore. I thought you understood that."

"I do understand," Maya replied, her voice trembling. "But understanding doesn't make it hurt any less. I can't keep waiting around, hoping for scraps of your time."

The conversation ended on a tense note, leaving Arjun feeling conflicted. He didn't want to lose Maya, but he also couldn't neglect his academic and extracurricular commitments. The strain began to take a toll on him, affecting his focus and performance.

As TechFusion approached, Arjun was stretched thin. He noticed a decline in his grades and felt a growing sense of anxiety. His relationship with Maya became increasingly strained, with frequent arguments and misunderstandings. The lack of communication and the mounting pressure left him feeling overwhelmed.

After the festival concluded, Arjun decided it was time to address the issues head-on. He took a day off from his responsibilities and invited Maya for a walk around the serene lake on campus. As they walked, he opened up about his struggles, expressing his guilt and regret over how things had turned out.

"Maya, I'm sorry for how things have been," Arjun began, his voice earnest. "I've been so caught up in everything that I didn't realize how much I was neglecting you. I know I haven't been fair to you."

Maya listened, her expression softening. "Arjun, I appreciate you saying that. I know you're under a lot of pressure, but I need to feel valued in this relationship. We both need to make an effort to find a balance."

Arjun nodded, realizing the truth in her words. "You're right. I need to be better at managing my time and making sure that you know how much you mean to me. Can we start over and try to find that balance together?"

Maya smiled, relief evident on her face. "I'd like that, Arjun. Let's work on this together."

From that point on, Arjun made a conscious effort to better manage his time and priorities. He scheduled regular study sessions and club meetings, ensuring that he also allocated time for Maya and their relationship. They established open lines of communication, discussing their needs and expectations more transparently.

The changes didn't happen overnight, but gradually, things began to improve. Arjun found that by being more organized and setting boundaries, he could balance his academic responsibilities, extracurricular activities, and relationship more effectively. He also learned the importance of self-care and taking breaks to recharge, which helped him maintain his focus and productivity.

As Arjun navigated these complexities, he realized that the struggles he faced were teaching him valuable lessons about love and relationships. He learned the importance of communication, trust, and making time for the people who mattered. He understood that relationships required effort and compromise from both sides and that it was essential to maintain a balance between personal and professional commitments.

The experience also strengthened his relationship with Maya. They grew closer, having weathered the storm together and emerged with a deeper understanding of each other. Their bond was stronger, built on a foundation of mutual respect and support.

However, as the demands of the final year intensified, Arjun found himself once again struggling to maintain the balance. His thesis project, combined with the pressures of placement preparations, left him with little time to spare. Maya, too, was facing her own set of challenges, and the strain began to show.

One evening, after a particularly gruelling day, Arjun returned to his room to find a note from Maya. She had written about her feelings of loneliness and frustration, and how she felt that they were growing apart despite their efforts. The note ended with a request to take a break and re-evaluate their relationship.

Arjun felt a pang of sadness as he read the note. He knew that Maya's feelings were valid, and that the pressures they were both facing had taken a toll on their relationship. He respected her decision and agreed that a break might be necessary for them to gain perspective and focus on their individual challenges.

During this break, Arjun threw himself into his studies and extracurricular commitments. He found solace in his friends, who provided support and understanding during this difficult time. The break allowed him to reflect on his relationship with Maya and understand the importance of balance and communication.

As the semester progressed, Arjun and Maya maintained a cordial relationship, occasionally meeting to catch up and offer support to each other. The break gave them both the space they needed to grow individually and focus on their personal goals. They found a new rhythm in their friendship, one that was based on mutual respect and understanding.

Arjun used this time to reflect deeply on what he had learned from his relationship with Maya. He understood the importance of being present, communicating openly, and making time for loved ones. These lessons extended beyond romantic relationships and influenced his interactions with friends, family, and even in professional settings.

One afternoon, while sitting by the campus lake where they had shared many heartfelt conversations, Arjun pondered the changes he had undergone. His relationship with Maya had taught him patience and the value of listening. He realized that his initial approach to relationships had been somewhat self-centred, focusing more on his own needs than on truly understanding his partner. This revelation was humbling, and it spurred a significant change in how he approached all his relationships.

Arjun began applying these lessons to his friendships. He became a more attentive and empathetic friend, often reaching out to check on others and offering support during stressful times. His friends noticed this change, and it strengthened their bonds. Arjun's ability to balance his own needs with those of others created a more harmonious social environment around him.

Academically, Arjun also thrived. He found that the skills he had developed in his relationship with Maya, such as patience, clear communication, and empathy, translated well into teamwork and collaborative projects. He became a reliable team member who could mediate conflicts and ensure that everyone's voice was heard. This not only improved his academic performance but also made him a respected figure among his peers.

One evening, while working on a group project in the library, Arjun reflected on the progress he had made. He realized that the growth he experienced was due in part to the lessons learned from his relationship with Maya. He had developed a more profound understanding of himself and what he valued in relationships.

As the end of the semester approached, Arjun and Maya decided to have one last meeting before their schedules became too hectic. They met at their favourite cafe on campus, a place filled with memories of their time together. The conversation flowed easily, and they both shared updates about their lives and future aspirations. It was clear that they had both grown significantly since their breakup.

"Maya, I've been thinking a lot about our time together," Arjun said, his voice thoughtful. "It taught me so much about what it means to be in a relationship. I've realized how important it is to truly listen and support each other."

Maya smiled, her eyes reflecting the same growth and maturity. "I've learned a lot too, Arjun. We were both figuring things out, and despite the challenges, I think we helped each other grow. I'm grateful for that."

Their conversation continued, filled with mutual respect and a sense of closure. They knew their paths were now different, but the experiences they shared had left an indelible mark on both of them. As they parted ways that evening, Arjun felt a sense of peace. He understood that their relationship had been a crucial part of his journey, helping him become a more well-rounded and resilient individual.

With the semester nearing its end, Arjun focused on his personal goals with renewed vigour. He looked forward to the future with a sense of excitement and confidence. The lessons he had learned from his relationship with Maya, combined with his academic and personal growth at NIT, had equipped him well for the challenges ahead.

Chapter 9: Coping with Homesickness

Arjun had always been close to his family. Growing up in a tight-knit household, he was accustomed to the constant presence of his parents and younger sister. When he first arrived at NIT, the excitement of a new beginning and the thrill of independence overshadowed the pangs of homesickness. But as the initial excitement faded and the realities of college life set in, Arjun began to feel the weight of being away from home.

The episodes of homesickness would often strike unexpectedly. Sometimes, it was a simple trigger – a familiar song, a favourite dish in the mess hall, or a call from his mother. Other times, it was the silence of his dorm room, the loneliness of late-night study sessions, or the overwhelming stress of exams and assignments. The emotional toll of missing his family began to weigh heavily on Arjun.

One particularly difficult evening, Arjun found himself sitting alone in his room, surrounded by textbooks and notes. The pressure of an upcoming exam and the isolation of his dorm hit him hard. He picked up his phone and dialled his mother's number, hoping to find some comfort in her voice.

"Hi, Mom," Arjun said, trying to keep his voice steady.

"Arjun, beta! How are you?" his mother's voice was warm and soothing, instantly bringing a sense of relief.

"I'm okay, just a bit stressed with exams coming up," Arjun admitted, his voice wavering slightly.

His mother sensed his distress. "It's normal to feel this way, Arjun. You're doing great, and we're all so proud of you. Just take it one step at a time. Remember, we're always here for you."

The conversation with his mother helped alleviate some of the homesickness, but Arjun knew he needed more strategies to cope with the emotional toll. He decided to take proactive steps to address his feelings and find a balance between his life at NIT and his connections back home.

One of the first strategies Arjun adopted was scheduling regular calls home. Every Sunday, without fail, he would call his family and catch up on their lives. These conversations became a lifeline, providing a sense of continuity and connection. He also made it a point to visit home during holidays and long weekends, cherishing the time spent with his loved ones.

Arjun also found solace in his friendships at NIT. He opened up to Suresh, Kavya, and Rajat about his feelings of homesickness. Sharing his struggles with them brought a sense of camaraderie and understanding. They, too, had their moments of missing home, and together, they found ways to support each other.

One evening, as they gathered in the common room, Arjun suggested, "Why don't we plan a small get-together for Diwali? We can cook some traditional dishes, light lamps, and celebrate together. It might help us feel a bit closer to home."

The idea was met with enthusiasm, and the group threw themselves into planning the celebration. They pooled their resources, bought ingredients, and spent hours in the kitchen, laughing and sharing stories as they cooked. When Diwali night arrived, the common room was filled with the aroma of homemade sweets and savoury dishes. The warm glow of lamp lit up the room, creating a festive atmosphere that reminded them of home.

As they sat together, enjoying the meal and the company, Arjun felt a sense of contentment. The celebration had brought a piece of home to NIT, and for that evening, the pangs of homesickness were replaced with joy and togetherness.

In addition to these efforts, Arjun immersed himself in college activities to keep his mind occupied. He continued to be actively involved in the Film and Music Society, organizing events and participating in various projects. He also joined the college cricket team, finding a sense of camaraderie and teamwork that helped alleviate his loneliness.

The support of his friends and the activities he engaged in provided a sense of belonging and purpose. However, there were still moments when the homesickness would resurface, reminding Arjun of the distance between him and his family.

One such moment occurred during the winter break. While most of his friends went home for the holidays, Arjun decided to stay back at NIT to work on a research project. The campus was eerily quiet, and the absence of his friends made the loneliness more pronounced.

On New Year's Eve, as he sat alone in his room, Arjun felt a deep ache in his chest. The celebrations and fireworks outside only amplified his sense of isolation. In a bid to distract himself, he opened his laptop and started browsing through old photos of family vacations and celebrations.

The memories brought a bittersweet smile to his face. He decided to call his family and wish them a Happy New Year. As he spoke to his parents and sister, he felt a wave of emotion wash over him. The conversation was filled with laughter, love, and reassurances, reminding Arjun that he was never truly alone.

Determined to make the most of his time at NIT, Arjun resolved to create new memories and experiences that would become cherished parts of his journey. He continued to engage in college activities, build strong relationships, and find joy in the little moments.

As the semester progressed, Arjun found that his strategies for coping with homesickness were becoming more effective. The regular calls home, visits during holidays, and the support of his friends provided a sense of stability and comfort. He also learned to embrace the solitude, using it as an opportunity for self-reflection and growth.

One day, as Arjun walked around the serene campus lake, he reflected on his journey. The homesickness that had once felt overwhelming had now become a manageable part of his life. He had found a balance between his connections back home and his life at NIT, learning to appreciate the beauty of both worlds.

Arjun realized that homesickness was a natural part of the experience, a testament to the love and bonds he had with his family. It had taught him the importance of resilience, adaptability, and finding joy in the present moment.

As he stood by the lake, watching the sunset, Arjun felt a sense of peace. He knew that the journey was far from over, but he was ready to face whatever challenges lay ahead. The experiences and lessons he had gained at NIT had shaped him into a stronger, more self-aware individual, ready to embrace the future with confidence and hope.

Arjun's reflections by the lake were interrupted by a soft, familiar voice. He turned to see Neha walking towards him, a warm smile on her face. "Hey, Arjun," she greeted him. "Mind if I join you?"

Arjun welcomed her presence, and they sat together, watching the sun dip below the horizon. Neha had always been a comforting presence in his life, and their conversations had a way of grounding him.

"I've been thinking a lot about home lately," Arjun admitted. "It's been tough balancing everything and dealing with the homesickness."

Neha nodded, her eyes reflecting understanding. "I get it, Arjun. I miss my family too. But I think it's important to create a sense of home here, with the people and experiences we have."

Her words resonated with Arjun. He realized that while he missed his family, he had also built a new family at NIT – a network of friends and mentors who supported and cared for him. This realization brought a sense of comfort and reassurance.

As they continued to talk, Arjun felt a renewed sense of purpose. He decided to take Neha's advice to heart and focus on creating a sense of home at NIT. He organized more gatherings and outings with his friends, finding joy in their shared experiences and deepening bonds.

One of the most memorable moments came during the college's annual cultural fest. Arjun, along with his friends, participated in various events and competitions, immersing themselves in the vibrant atmosphere. The fest provided a welcome distraction from the stress of academics and a chance to celebrate their camaraderie.

Arjun also made an effort to explore the local culture and surroundings. He and his friends took weekend trips to nearby towns and attractions, discovering new places and creating lasting memories. These adventures not only provided a break from the routine but also helped Arjun appreciate the beauty and diversity of his new environment.

Throughout these experiences, Arjun learned to find a balance between his life at NIT and his connections back home. He realized that homesickness was a natural part of the journey, but it didn't have to define his experience. By embracing his new surroundings and nurturing his relationships, he could create a sense of belonging and fulfilment.

One evening, as Arjun sat in his room, he received a video call from his family. His mother's smiling face appeared on the screen, followed by his father's and sister's.

"Hi, Arjun! We miss you!" his sister exclaimed, her excitement palpable.

Arjun's heart swelled with love and gratitude. "I miss you all too," he replied, a smile spreading across his face. "But I'm doing well here. I've made some great friends and had some amazing experiences."

The conversation flowed easily, filled with laughter and updates on their lives. Arjun felt a sense of connection that transcended the physical distance. His family remained a pillar of support, and their love gave him the strength to face the challenges ahead.

As the call ended, Arjun sat back, reflecting on his journey. He had come a long way since those initial days of homesickness and loneliness. He had learned to navigate the complexities of college life, build meaningful relationships, and find joy in the present moment.

Arjun knew that the road ahead would have its ups and downs, but he was ready to face it with resilience and optimism. The experiences and lessons he had gained at NIT had shaped him into a stronger, more self-aware individual, prepared to embrace the future with confidence.

With a heart full of hope and a mind ready for new adventures, Arjun continued his journey at NIT, determined to thrive and succeed. The experiences and achievements of his time at NIT were just the beginning, and he was ready to take on the world with confidence and determination. The future was bright, and Arjun was ready to embrace it with open arms, knowing that he had the skills, support, and resilience to succeed.

Arjun's journey at NIT was a testament to his growth and adaptability. He had faced the emotional toll of homesickness, navigated the complexities of friendships and relationships, and emerged stronger for it. With the support of his family and friends, and the lessons he had learned along the way, Arjun was ready to take on whatever challenges the future held.

Chapter 10: Proxies and Hostel Friendship

Arjun had quickly become familiar with the culture of proxies at NIT. The concept was simple: students would sign attendance for their absent friends, helping them avoid penalties for missing classes. While it seemed like a harmless way to help each other out, the practice was fraught with risks and ethical dilemmas.

The first time Arjun encountered the idea of proxies was during a particularly boring lecture on thermodynamics. His friend Rajat leaned over and whispered, "Hey, can you mark me present tomorrow? I've got a cricket practice session."

Arjun hesitated. "Isn't that risky? What if we get caught?"

Rajat shrugged. "Everyone does it. Just make sure you get my roll number right."

Arjun agreed reluctantly, marking Rajat's name on the attendance sheet the next day. The thrill of getting away with it was quickly overshadowed by a sense of unease. He couldn't shake the feeling that he was compromising his integrity.

Despite his reservations, the practice of proxies became a common occurrence among his friends. They would cover for each other during lectures, labs, and even exams. The system relied heavily on trust and mutual understanding. If one person got caught, it could spell trouble for everyone involved.

One evening, as Arjun sat in his dorm room, he overheard a conversation between his hostel mates, Suresh and Kavya. They were discussing the upcoming midterms and how they planned to use proxies to manage their study schedules.

"I'll cover for you in the morning classes if you take care of my afternoon labs," Suresh suggested.

Kavya nodded. "Deal. Just make sure you don't mess up the signatures."

Arjun joined the conversation, feeling a mix of curiosity and concern. "Aren't you worried about getting caught?"

Suresh chuckled. "It's all part of the game, Arjun. Besides, we've got each other's backs."

The camaraderie and trust among his hostel mates were undeniable. They supported each other through thick and thin, sharing notes, helping with assignments, and covering for each other during classes. The bond they shared extended beyond academics, encompassing late-night conversations, pranks, and deep friendships.

One night, as Arjun lay in bed, unable to sleep, he heard a knock on his door. It was Neha, looking distressed. "Arjun, can we talk?"

Arjun invited her in, sensing her need for support. They sat on his bed, and Neha opened up about the pressure she was feeling. "I'm struggling to keep up with everything. The classes, the projects, the exams... it's all too much."

Arjun listened attentively, offering words of comfort and reassurance. "You're not alone, Neha. We're all in this together. If you need help, just ask. We'll get through this."

Their conversation continued late into the night, with Arjun sharing his own struggles and fears. The vulnerability and honesty they shared strengthened their bond, creating a sense of trust and mutual support.

As the semester progressed, Arjun found himself increasingly reliant on the support of his hostel mates. They would gather in the common room for late-night study sessions, fueled by endless cups of tea and Maggi noodles. The camaraderie and trust among them created a sense of belonging and security.

The pranks and antics they indulged in added a touch of fun and laughter to their lives. From hiding each other's belongings to staging elaborate practical jokes, the hostel was a constant hub of activity and mischief. One memorable night, they decided to pull a prank on Rajat, who had a habit of falling asleep during their study sessions.

As Rajat dozed off on the couch, Arjun and Suresh carefully placed a fake spider on his chest. The moment Rajat woke up and saw the spider, he let out a loud scream, causing everyone to burst into laughter. The prank became a legendary story, retold countless times with exaggerated details.

Despite the fun and camaraderie, the risks associated with proxies loomed large. One day, during a particularly strict professor's lecture, Arjun's heart sank as the professor announced a surprise attendance check.

"Today, we're going to verify the attendance records," the professor declared, his eyes scanning the room. "If anyone is found to have marked a proxy, there will be serious consequences."

Arjun's mind raced. He had marked Rajat's name earlier that day, and the thought of getting caught filled him with dread. As the professor called out names and checked each student's ID, Arjun's anxiety grew.

When the professor reached Rajat's name, Arjun felt his palms grow sweaty. Rajat wasn't in class, and Arjun knew that if the professor discovered the proxy, it could mean trouble for both of them.

To Arjun's immense relief, the professor moved on without further scrutiny. The close call served as a stark reminder of the risks involved in using proxies. It was a wake-up call for Arjun, highlighting the importance of integrity and the potential consequences of compromising it.

The experience prompted Arjun to re-evaluate his approach to proxies. He realized that while the practice was widespread, it wasn't worth the risk or the ethical compromise. He decided to be more cautious and to prioritize his academic integrity.

Arjun's resolve was put to the test when Kavya approached him one day, asking for a proxy. "I have an important meeting for the cultural fest. Can you mark me present in the lab?"

Arjun hesitated, feeling torn between helping a friend and maintaining his integrity. "Kavya, I don't think I can do it anymore. It's too risky, and I don't want to compromise my values."

Kavya looked disappointed but understood his stance. "I get it, Arjun. Thanks for being honest. I'll figure something out."

The decision to refrain from using proxies was a turning point for Arjun. It strengthened his sense of integrity and reinforced his commitment to honesty. It also deepened his friendships, as his hostel mates respected his choice and continued to support him.

As the semester continued, Arjun's relationships with his hostel mates grew stronger. The late-night conversations, shared experiences, and mutual trust created a sense of family within the hostel. They celebrated each other's successes, provided comfort during difficult times, and stood by each other through thick and thin.

One evening, as they sat on the rooftop, enjoying the cool breeze and gazing at the stars, Arjun reflected on the journey they had shared. "You guys have become my second family," he said, his voice filled with emotion. "I can't imagine going through this journey without you."

Suresh raised his cup of tea in a toast. "To friendship and the bonds we've built. Here's to many more memories and adventures together."

The group clinked their cups together, feeling a profound sense of connection and gratitude. The friendships they had forged at NIT were more than just casual acquaintances; they were deep, meaningful relationships that would last a lifetime.

As the semester came to an end, Arjun looked back on his experiences with a sense of fulfilment. The culture of proxies had taught him valuable lessons about integrity and trust, while the camaraderie and bonds formed with his hostel mates had enriched his life in countless ways.

Arjun knew that the journey was far from over, but he felt ready to face whatever challenges lay ahead. The friendships and experiences he had gained at NIT had shaped him into a stronger, more self-aware individual, ready to embrace the future with confidence and hope.

With a heart full of hope and a mind ready for new adventures, Arjun continued his journey at NIT, determined to thrive and succeed. The experiences and achievements of his time at NIT were just the beginning, and he was ready to take on the world with confidence and determination. The future was bright, and Arjun was ready to embrace it with open arms, knowing that he had the skills, support, and resilience to succeed.

Chapter 11: The Startup Challenge

Arjun sat in the bustling common room, flipping through a magazine, when a bright, colourful flyer on the noticeboard caught his eye. It announced an upcoming event that piqued his interest: "The NIT Startup Challenge." The challenge invited teams to develop innovative startup ideas and present them to a panel of industry experts. The winning team would receive funding and mentorship to bring their idea to life.

Arjun's heart raced with excitement. This was an opportunity to apply his engineering knowledge, entrepreneurial spirit, and creativity in a real-world setting. He quickly shared the idea with his friends, Rajat, Suresh, and Kavya, who were equally enthusiastic about participating.

The first step was forming their team officially and brainstorming ideas. They gathered in their favourite spot in the library, surrounded by notebooks, laptops, and a whiteboard filled with scribbles. The atmosphere was charged with creativity and excitement as they threw around various ideas.

Kavya suggested, "How about developing a smart energy management system for homes? With the increasing emphasis on sustainability, it could be a game-changer."

Suresh, always the tech wizard, added, "We could integrate it with IoT devices to monitor and optimize energy usage in real-time."

Rajat, thinking practically, chimed in, "And we could offer an app that provides users with insights and tips on reducing their energy consumption."

Arjun loved the idea. It was innovative, practical, and had the potential to make a significant impact. They decided to move forward with it, excited about the possibilities.

The next few weeks were a whirlwind of activity. The team divided tasks based on their strengths. Arjun focused on the overall project management, ensuring that they stayed on track with their timeline. Kavya worked on market research, identifying the target audience and potential competitors. Suresh and Rajat delved into the technical aspects, designing the smart system and developing the app.

They spent countless hours in the library and labs, researching, designing, and refining their idea. They also attended workshops organized by the college's entrepreneurship cell, gaining valuable insights into business planning, pitching, and marketing.

As the competition day approached, the team worked tirelessly to create a working prototype of their smart energy management system. They faced numerous challenges, from technical glitches to time constraints, but their determination kept them going.

They set up a test environment in their hostel room, connecting various IoT devices to their system and monitoring its performance. There were moments of frustration when things didn't work as expected, but each setback was a learning experience. With persistence and teamwork, they finally had a functional prototype.

With the prototype ready, it was time to prepare their pitch. Arjun took the lead, creating a compelling presentation that highlighted the problem they were addressing, their innovative solution, and the potential impact. Kavya worked on the financial projections, ensuring they had a solid business model. Suresh and Rajat prepared a live demonstration of the prototype.

They practiced their pitch repeatedly, fine-tuning their delivery and anticipating questions from the judges. The more they practiced, the more confident they became.

On the day of the competition, the campus was buzzing with excitement. Teams from various colleges had gathered, each with their unique ideas and prototypes. The atmosphere was electric with anticipation.

Arjun and his team were nervous but confident. They knew they had put in the hard work and were ready to showcase their idea. When their turn came, they walked onto the stage with a mix of excitement and nerves.

Arjun started the pitch, introducing the problem and their innovative solution. Kavya followed with the market analysis and business model, while Suresh and Rajat conducted the live demonstration. The prototype worked flawlessly, and the audience was impressed.

The judges asked several questions, challenging their assumptions and projections. The team handled each question with poise, demonstrating their thorough understanding and preparation.

After all the presentations, the judges deliberated and finally announced the results. Arjun and his team held their breath as the names were called. When their project was declared the winner, they erupted in cheers, hugging each other in disbelief and joy.

"This is incredible!" Kavya exclaimed, tears of happiness in her eyes.

Arjun felt a profound sense of accomplishment. This victory was not just about winning a competition; it was a testament to their teamwork, innovation, and perseverance.

Back in their hostel room that night, the team celebrated their victory with laughter and shared memories. They reflected on the journey, from the initial brainstorming sessions to the sleepless nights in the lab.

"This experience has taught us so much," Suresh said. "Not just about technology and business, but about working together and pushing our limits."

Arjun nodded in agreement. "We've proven that we can take on any challenge. Let's keep this momentum going and see how far we can take this project."

The NIT Startup Challenge had been a transformative experience for Arjun and his friends. It reinforced their passion for engineering and innovation and strengthened their bond as a team. As they looked ahead, they knew that this was just the beginning of their entrepreneurial journey. With newfound confidence and a shared vision, they were ready to take on the world, one innovative idea at a time.

Chapter 12: The Midway Crisis

Arjun had always been a diligent student. Throughout his time at NIT, he managed to balance his coursework, extracurricular activities, and social life with a level of competence that earned him respect among his peers. However, as the semester reached its midpoint, the pressure of mid-semester exams and project deadlines began to mount, pushing Arjun to his limits.

The signs of impending burnout were subtle at first. Arjun noticed himself becoming more irritable, his concentration waning during lectures, and his usual enthusiasm for group activities diminishing. The sleepless nights spent poring over textbooks and working on projects began to take a toll on his physical and mental well-being.

One particularly gruelling week, Arjun found himself facing a series of back-to-back exams and a major project deadline. The weight of these commitments felt crushing, and despite his best efforts, he struggled to keep up. As the week progressed, the stress became unbearable, culminating in a significant academic setback during his thermodynamics exam.

Arjun had always been confident in his understanding of the subject, but as he stared at the exam paper, his mind went blank. Panic set in as he realized he couldn't recall key concepts and equations. His hands trembled as he attempted to answer the questions, but each response felt more uncertain than the last. By the time the exam ended, Arjun was overwhelmed with a sense of failure.

The results confirmed his worst fears. Arjun's grade for the thermodynamics exam was far below his usual standards, a stark reminder of the pressure and burnout he had been experiencing. The setback hit him hard, shaking his confidence and leaving him grappling with feelings of inadequacy and fear of failure.

That evening, Arjun retreated to his dorm room, his mind a whirlwind of self-doubt and frustration. He sat on his bed, staring at the exam paper, replaying the mistakes in his mind. The room felt suffocating, the silence amplifying his inner turmoil. Unable to contain his emotions, Arjun reached out to his mentor, Professor Sharma. He had always admired Professor Sharma's wisdom and approachability, and he hoped that seeking guidance would help him navigate this challenging period.

"Professor, I don't know what happened," Arjun admitted during their meeting. "I thought I was prepared, but I completely blanked out during the exam. I feel like I'm failing."

Professor Sharma listened attentively, his expression one of understanding and concern. "Arjun, it's clear that you've been under a lot of pressure. It's important to recognize that setbacks are a part of the learning process. What matters is how you respond to them."

Arjun nodded, feeling a glimmer of hope. "But how do I get back on track? I feel like I'm drowning."

Professor Sharma leaned forward, his gaze steady. "First, take a step back and reflect on what's been causing this burnout. Identify the factors contributing to your stress and find ways to address them. Don't hesitate to seek support from your peers and mentors. Remember, you're not alone in this journey."

Arjun left the meeting with a sense of clarity and determination. He realized that he needed to take proactive steps to manage his stress and regain his focus. The first step was to address the physical toll that burnout had taken on him. He committed to a more balanced routine, incorporating regular exercise, adequate sleep, and healthier eating habits.

Next, Arjun sought support from his friends, confiding in Suresh, Kavya, and Rajat about his struggles, sharing his fears and frustrations. Their responses were overwhelmingly supportive, offering empathy and encouragement.

"Arjun, we've all been there," Suresh said, patting him on the back. "You're one of the smartest guys I know. This is just a bump in the road."

Kavya nodded in agreement. "Let's work together to get through this. We can help each other with study sessions and make sure no one falls behind."

Their solidarity and encouragement gave Arjun a renewed sense of purpose. They organized group study sessions, creating a supportive environment where they could tackle difficult concepts together and keep each other motivated. The late-night study sessions, once a source of stress, became an opportunity for camaraderie and mutual support.

Despite his efforts to maintain a balanced routine, Arjun often found himself awake in the middle of the night, his mind racing with worries and fears about his academic performance. The pressure to excel, coupled with the fear of failure, created a constant state of anxiety that left him feeling drained and exhausted.

One particularly difficult night, he decided to take a walk around the campus to clear his mind. The cool night air provided a temporary respite from the suffocating pressure he felt. As he wandered aimlessly, he stumbled upon a bench near the serene campus lake. He sat down, the silence of the night amplifying the thoughts swirling in his mind.

"Why am I struggling so much?" he thought to himself, the frustration evident in his expression. "I used to be so confident, so sure of myself. What changed?"

The reflection on his struggles brought a flood of emotions. Tears welled up in his eyes as he grappled with the weight of his expectations and the fear of letting himself and his family down. The tears flowed freely, a cathartic release of the pent-up stress and anxiety he had been carrying.

In that moment of vulnerability, he realized the importance of self-compassion. He had been so focused on achieving perfection that he had forgotten to acknowledge his own humanity. The setback he faced was not a reflection of his worth, but rather an opportunity for growth and learning.

The next day, with a renewed sense of purpose, Arjun decided to seek additional support. He reached out to the campus counselling centre, recognizing the need for professional guidance to navigate the mental and emotional challenges he was facing. The counsellor he spoke with provided valuable insights and coping strategies, helping him develop a healthier mindset towards his academic journey.

One of the key takeaways from the counselling sessions was the importance of setting realistic goals and managing expectations. He learned to break down his tasks into manageable chunks, celebrating small victories along the way. This approach not only alleviated the overwhelming sense of pressure but also allowed him to appreciate his progress.

Additionally, Arjun began to explore new hobbies and interests to manage his stress. He joined a meditation group on campus, which taught him techniques to calm his mind and centre his thoughts. This practice became a daily routine, helping him to stay grounded amid the chaos of academic life. Furthermore, he rediscovered his passion for music, spending time playing the guitar and writing songs, which provided a creative outlet for his emotions.

These activities, along with the ongoing support from his friends, helped Arjun build a balanced and fulfilling routine. They devised a study schedule that balanced individual efforts with group support, ensuring that no one felt isolated or overwhelmed. The camaraderie and shared commitment to their academic goals created a positive and motivating environment.

In addition to his friends' support, Arjun sought help from other professors and mentors. He attended additional office hours, asked questions, and sought clarification on topics he found challenging. The willingness of his professors to provide guidance and support reassured him that he was not alone in his academic journey.

One of the most transformative moments came during a conversation with Professor Rao, his project advisor. Professor Rao had a reputation for being strict but fair, and Arjun had always admired his dedication to his students.

"Arjun, I've seen your potential from the beginning," Professor Rao said during their meeting. "This setback doesn't define you. Use it as an opportunity to learn and grow. Focus on your strengths, and don't be afraid to ask for help when you need it."

The words resonated deeply with Arjun. He realized that he had been placing immense pressure on himself to excel without acknowledging the importance of seeking support and learning from setbacks. With a renewed mindset, Arjun approached his studies with a sense of resilience and determination.

As the weeks passed, Arjun's efforts began to pay off. He saw gradual improvements in his grades and felt more confident in his understanding of the subjects. The project that had once seemed insurmountable became a manageable task, thanks to the guidance of Professor Rao and the support of his friends.

The experience also prompted Arjun to reflect on his priorities and time management. He recognized the importance of maintaining a balance between academics and personal well-being. He made time for activities that brought him joy and relaxation, such as playing cricket, listening to music, and spending time with his friends.

One evening, as Arjun and his friends sat in the common room, sharing stories and laughter, he felt a profound sense of gratitude. The journey had been challenging, but it had also brought them closer together and taught them valuable lessons about resilience, support, and the importance of friendship.

As the semester drew to a close, Arjun's academic performance had improved significantly. He had not only overcome the setback but had also gained a deeper understanding of himself and his capabilities. The experience had strengthened his resolve and taught him the importance of seeking help, maintaining balance, and embracing challenges as opportunities for growth.

Arjun's journey through the midway crisis was a testament to his resilience and adaptability. He had faced the pressures of exams and deadlines, navigated the challenges of academic setbacks, and emerged stronger for it. With the support of his friends, mentors, and the lessons he had learned, Arjun felt ready to take on whatever challenges the future held.

Arjun felt a renewed sense of purpose and drive as he looked forward to his continued journey at NIT. He knew that his time there had equipped him with the knowledge and experience necessary to face the world's challenges. Arjun was eager to apply what he had learned, to innovate, and to make a meaningful impact.

Chapter 13: The Night Canteen Chronicles

The night canteen at NIT was a legendary spot on campus, known for its late-night snacks, bustling atmosphere, and the best stuffed parathas around. For Arjun and his friends, it was a sanctuary—a place where they could unwind after long hours of studying, laugh about the day's events, and enjoy delicious food.

One particularly hectic week, as the group was buried under piles of books and assignments, Suresh proposed a much-needed break. "Guys, we need to hit the night canteen. I can't handle another minute of thermodynamics without some parathas."

Kavya immediately agreed, her eyes lighting up at the thought. "Yes! And we can catch up with some of the seniors. They always have the best stories."

Rajat, who had been staring at his laptop for hours, finally looked up and grinned. "Count me in. I need food and a good laugh."

Arjun, feeling the pressure of an impending project deadline, hesitated for a moment but then nodded. "Alright, let's do it. We deserve a break."

As they made their way to the night canteen, the air was filled with the familiar sounds of laughter and conversations. The canteen was packed, as usual, with students taking a breather from their studies. The aroma of freshly cooked parathas wafted through the air, making their mouths water.

They found a table and ordered a round of stuffed parathas—paneer, aloo, and gobi—along with steaming cups of tea. Just as they were settling in, a group of seniors joined their table. Among them was Anil, a final-year student known for his hilarious anecdotes and mischievous pranks.

"Mind if we join you guys?" Anil asked, already pulling up a chair.

"Not at all," Arjun replied, glad for the extra company. "We could use some entertainment."

Anil grinned and leaned in, ready to share his latest tale. "So, did I ever tell you guys about the time we rigged the electrical lab's circuit board?"

Kavya's eyes widened with curiosity. "No, but I have a feeling this is going to be good."

Anil launched into the story, animatedly describing how he and his friends had decided to play a prank on their strictest professor, Dr. Rao. They had rigged the circuit board to play a recorded message whenever it was switched on, mimicking Dr. Rao's voice lecturing about Ohm's Law.

"We timed it perfectly," Anil said, laughing at the memory. "Dr. Rao walked in, switched on the board, and suddenly heard his own voice booming out of the speakers. He looked so confused and kept adjusting his glasses, thinking he was hearing things."

Rajat nearly choked on his tea, laughing. "That's brilliant! How did he react when he realized it was a prank?"

Anil chuckled. "He wasn't mad, surprisingly. He actually appreciated the ingenuity. Said it was the most creative application of circuits he'd seen in years."

As the laughter died down, Kavya asked, "Any other legendary pranks or funny moments we should know about?"

Anil nodded, a mischievous gleam in his eye. "Oh, there are plenty. Like the time we convinced the entire first-year batch that the campus library had a secret underground section with ancient engineering texts."

Suresh raised an eyebrow. "Did they believe it?"

"Absolutely," Anil said, grinning. "We even staged a fake discovery, complete with 'ancient' books we'd aged with coffee and tea stains. The first-years spent weeks trying to find the secret entrance."

Arjun shook his head, laughing. "I can't believe they fell for it. You guys are something else."

Their parathas arrived, and the conversation shifted to the food. The stuffed parathas were as delicious as ever, and the group ate with gusto, savouring every bite.

Between mouthfuls, Kavya asked, "What's the craziest thing that's happened at the night canteen?"

Anil thought for a moment, a smile playing on his lips. "Probably the night we had an impromptu debate competition. It started with just a casual argument about which engineering branch is the toughest, and before we knew it, the entire canteen was divided into teams, passionately defending their fields."

Rajat leaned in, intrigued. "Who won?"

"Nobody, really," Anil said with a laugh. "It turned into a hilarious free-for-all. People were coming up with the most ridiculous arguments, and it ended with everyone agreeing that all branches had their own unique tortures."

Suresh chuckled. "Sounds like the kind of night we could use right now. A little distraction from all the stress."

The conversation drifted into stories of past canteen escapades. Anil regaled them with the tale of how they once convinced a gullible junior that the canteen had a secret menu accessible only at midnight, which supposedly included dishes with magical properties.

"He showed up at midnight for a week, asking for things like 'the invisibility curry' and 'the wisdom noodles'," Anil said, barely able to contain his laughter. "The canteen staff eventually caught on and played along, serving him regular food with fancy names."

Arjun and his friends laughed, imagining the bewildered junior's face. "I can't believe he fell for that!" Kavya said, wiping tears of laughter from her eyes.

As the evening wore on, the canteen started to empty out, but Arjun and his friends lingered, enjoying the rare respite. The seniors continued to share more stories, each one funnier than the last. It felt good to laugh, to forget about the mounting pressures and just enjoy the moment.

Arjun glanced around the canteen, taking in the warm lights, the chatter, and the clinking of dishes. This place had become a second home, a refuge where they could be themselves. He felt a pang of nostalgia, realizing that their time here was coming to an end.

"Do you remember the time when we had that surprise quiz in the middle of the night?" Rajat asked, turning to Anil.

Anil nodded. "Oh, how could I forget? Dr. Menon was notorious for his pop quizzes. That night, he decided to test us on topics we hadn't even covered yet. Everyone rushed to the canteen afterward, desperate for some comfort food and a place to vent."

Kavya laughed. "I remember that! We all huddled together, frantically discussing answers and trying to make sense of the questions."

Suresh added, "And then someone suggested we play charades to lighten the mood. It was one of the best nights here."

Anil nodded, smiling. "The canteen has seen its share of highs and lows. It's amazing how a place like this can become the backdrop for so many memories."

As they ordered another round of tea, the conversation took a reflective turn. They talked about their dreams, their fears, and their plans for the future. The seniors offered advice, sharing their own experiences and the lessons they had learned along the way.

Arjun felt a deep sense of gratitude. These were the moments that made college life special—the late-night talks, the shared laughter, and the bonds that formed over countless cups of tea and plates of parathas.

"Thank you for sharing your stories," Arjun said, raising his cup in a toast. "To the night canteen, and to the memories we've made here."

"Cheers!" everyone echoed, clinking their cups together.

As they finally decided to call it a night, they walked back to their hostel, the cool night air refreshing against their faces. Arjun felt lighter, the stress of the week melting away. He knew that no matter where life took them, they would always have these moments to look back on.

The night canteen had not just been a place to eat; it had been a place to connect, to laugh, and to celebrate the joys of engineering life. It was these little moments that made their journey at NIT truly special.

With the memories of the evening fresh in their minds, they returned to their studies with a renewed sense of purpose. The night canteen chronicles would be a cherished part of their college experience, a reminder of the friendships they had forged and the laughter they had shared.

As they prepared for the final stretch of their college journey, they knew that the bonds they had formed at the night canteen would last a lifetime. And no matter where they went, they would always carry a piece of NIT with them, along with the countless stories and memories created over cups of tea and plates of stuffed parathas.

Chapter 14: Internships and Industry Exposure

Arjun Mehra stood at a crossroads as the semester progressed. With the pressures of midterms behind him, a new challenge loomed on the horizon: securing a summer internship. The hunt for internships was a crucial step for students at NIT, offering them a chance to gain practical industry experience and enhance their resumes.

The application process was intense and competitive. Arjun found himself spending countless hours polishing his resume, writing cover letters, and preparing for interviews. The pressure to secure a prestigious internship weighed heavily on him, and self-doubt crept in as he compared himself to his peers.

"Will I be able to get a good internship?" Arjun wondered, staring at his computer screen filled with job listings. The uncertainty gnawed at him, but he knew that perseverance was key.

Arjun's first step was to seek guidance from the college's career services office. He scheduled a meeting with Mrs. Kapoor, the career counsellor, who had a reputation for providing valuable insights and support to students.

"Arjun, it's great to see you taking the initiative," Mrs. Kapoor said as they sat down for their meeting. "Let's start by reviewing your resume and discussing your career goals."

As they went through his resume, Mrs. Kapoor provided constructive feedback, helping Arjun highlight his strengths and experiences. She also suggested networking with alumni and attending industry seminars to gain a better understanding of potential opportunities.

"Remember, Arjun," Mrs. Kapoor advised, "the internship hunt is a learning experience in itself. Stay persistent and open to various opportunities. Every experience, whether successful or not, will contribute to your growth."

With a refined resume and a clearer sense of direction, Arjun began applying to various companies. He faced multiple rejections, each one a blow to his confidence. However, he reminded himself of Mrs. Kapoor's words and continued to apply, determined to secure an internship.

One evening, as Arjun sat in the common room with Suresh, Kavya, and Rajat, he received an email notification. It was from a well-known tech company, inviting him for an interview. His heart raced with excitement and nerves.

"Guys, I got an interview!" Arjun exclaimed, unable to contain his excitement.

"That's amazing, Arjun!" Kavya said, giving him a high-five. "You'll do great. Just be yourself and showcase your skills."

The interview preparation consumed Arjun's thoughts and time. He researched the company, practiced common interview questions, and even participated in mock interviews with his friends. The support and encouragement from his friends bolstered his confidence.

The day of the interview arrived, and Arjun felt a mix of excitement and anxiety. Dressed in a crisp shirt and tie, he entered the company's office, his mind focused on making a positive impression.

The interview went smoothly, with Arjun confidently discussing his academic achievements, technical skills, and extracurricular activities. He also highlighted his involvement in the Film and Music Society and the electrical engineering club he had founded.

A week later, Arjun received the news he had been hoping for: he had secured the internship. The sense of accomplishment was overwhelming, and he couldn't wait to share the news with his friends.

"Guys, I got the internship!" Arjun announced, beaming with pride.

Suresh, Kavya, and Rajat erupted in cheers, congratulating him on his success. The journey had been challenging, but the reward was worth the effort.

As summer approached, Arjun prepared for his internship, eager to gain practical industry experience. The first day at the tech company was a mix of excitement and nerves. The professional environment was vastly different from the academic setting, and Arjun had to adapt quickly.

He was assigned to a team working on a cutting-edge project involving artificial intelligence. The initial days were overwhelming as he familiarized himself with the company's workflow, tools, and technologies. However, his teammates were supportive, providing guidance and encouragement.

Arjun's mentor, Mr. Sharma, played a crucial role in his learning process. Mr. Sharma was a seasoned professional with years of experience in the industry, and his mentorship provided Arjun with valuable insights and knowledge.

"Arjun, focus on understanding the fundamentals and don't hesitate to ask questions," Mr. Sharma advised during one of their meetings. "The key to success in this field is continuous learning and adaptability."

Arjun took Mr. Sharma's words to heart, immersing himself in the project and absorbing as much knowledge as he could. He attended team meetings, participated in brainstorming sessions, and contributed his ideas and solutions. The hands-on experience was invaluable, allowing him to apply theoretical concepts to real-world problems.

Balancing the demands of the internship with his academic responsibilities was challenging. Arjun often found himself working late into the night, juggling project deadlines and coursework. However, the experience taught him the importance of time management and prioritization.

One evening, as Arjun worked on a particularly complex task, he received a message from Suresh. "Hey, we're grabbing dinner at the canteen. Join us?"

Arjun hesitated, torn between his work and the desire to spend time with his friends. Realizing the importance of balance, he decided to take a break and join them.

As they sat in the canteen, sharing stories and laughter, Arjun felt a sense of relief. The support and camaraderie of his friends provided a much-needed respite from the pressures of work and academics.

"Thanks for dragging me out, guys," Arjun said, smiling. "I needed this."

Kavya nodded. "It's important to take breaks, Arjun. We all need to recharge."

The summer flew by, and Arjun's internship experience exceeded his expectations. He gained practical skills, built professional relationships, and developed a deeper understanding of the industry. The challenges he faced and the lessons he learned were invaluable, shaping his perspective and aspirations.

However, just as Arjun began to feel confident in his abilities, a twist occurred that tested his resilience. Midway through his internship, the company announced a major reorganization. Arjun's team was dissolved, and he was reassigned to a different project with a new team. The sudden change was disorienting, and Arjun struggled to adapt to the new environment.

His new project involved working on a complex software system, an area he was less familiar with. The pressure to perform and prove himself in the new team was immense. Arjun found himself working longer hours, trying to catch up and understand the intricacies of the project.

The transition was tough, and Arjun's confidence took a hit. He felt like an outsider in the new team, struggling to find his footing. The fear of failure resurfaced, and he questioned his abilities.

One evening, as Arjun sat in the office, staring at his computer screen, he felt overwhelmed by the enormity of the task ahead. The familiar feelings of self-doubt and inadequacy crept in, threatening to derail his progress.

In a moment of desperation, Arjun decided to call Mr. Sharma for advice. "Mr. Sharma, I'm really struggling with this new project. I feel like I'm out of my depth."

Mr. Sharma's voice was calm and reassuring. "Arjun, it's natural to feel this way during transitions. Remember, every challenge is an opportunity to learn and grow. Take it one step at a time, and don't be afraid to ask for help from your new teammates. You have the skills and determination to succeed."

Mr. Sharma's words provided a sense of comfort and clarity. Arjun realized that he needed to approach the new project with the same perseverance and adaptability that had helped him secure the internship. He decided to seek guidance from his new teammates and learn from their expertise.

Over the next few weeks, Arjun focused on building relationships with his new team members. He attended team meetings, asked questions, and offered his assistance on various tasks. Gradually, he began to understand the complexities of the project and contribute effectively.

The turning point came when Arjun successfully debugged a critical issue in the software system. His team recognized his efforts, and he received praise from his new supervisor. The experience boosted his confidence and reinforced his belief in his abilities.

As the internship came to an end, Arjun reflected on the journey. The unexpected twist had tested his resilience, but it had also provided valuable lessons about adaptability and perseverance. He had navigated the challenges, built professional relationships, and gained practical skills that would serve him well in the future.

Back at NIT, Arjun resumed his academic responsibilities with renewed vigour. The balance he had learned to maintain during his internship carried over into his studies, allowing him to manage his time effectively and excel in his coursework.

One evening, as Arjun and his friends sat in the common room, he shared his reflections on the internship experience. "The internship was challenging, but it taught me so much about resilience and adaptability. I'm grateful for the opportunity and the support you all provided."

Suresh raised his cup of tea in a toast. "To internships and the lessons they bring. Here's to our growth and future success."

The group clinked their cups together, feeling a profound sense of connection and accomplishment. The journey had been challenging, but the experiences and lessons they had gained were invaluable.

As the semester progressed, Arjun continued to build on the skills and knowledge he had acquired during his internship. He applied his newfound insights to his projects and coursework, achieving academic success and personal growth.

Arjun's journey through the internship experience was a testament to his perseverance and adaptability. He had faced the challenges of securing an internship, navigating a professional environment, and balancing his responsibilities with resilience and determination. The support of his friends, mentors, and the lessons he had learned had shaped him into a more confident and capable individual.

As Arjun stood at the threshold of a new chapter, a surge of excitement and anticipation swept over him. The path ahead was cloaked in uncertainty, but he felt confident in his strength and resolve to overcome whatever challenges awaited.

Chapter 15: The Cultural Festival

The cultural festival at NIT was the most anticipated event of the year, a time when the entire campus came alive with music, dance, drama, and a plethora of other activities. For Arjun and his friends, it was a welcome break from their rigorous academic schedules and an opportunity to showcase their talents and unwind.

This year, the festival was bigger than ever, with participants from other NITs and local colleges joining in the celebrations. The influx of new faces added an extra layer of excitement and competition, pushing everyone to bring their best performances and ideas to the table.

Arjun had always been passionate about music, and this year, he decided to form a band with Rajat, Kavya, and Suresh. They had spent weeks rehearsing in the music room, perfecting their setlist and preparing for their performance at the festival. Their band, aptly named "Euphonic Beats," was a blend of various genres, reflecting their diverse tastes in music.

The days leading up to the festival were a whirlwind of activity. The campus was adorned with colourful decorations, and the air buzzed with excitement. Students scurried around, setting up stalls, arranging props, and rehearsing for their respective performances. The sense of camaraderie and shared enthusiasm was palpable.

One evening, as the group was taking a break from rehearsals, they sat on the steps outside the auditorium, enjoying the cool breeze. "I can't believe the festival is finally here," Kavya said, her eyes sparkling with excitement. "We've worked so hard for this."

Suresh nodded, adjusting the strap of his guitar. "It's going to be epic. We've put in the effort, and now it's time to enjoy and give it our best shot."

Rajat, always the motivator, added, "Remember, it's not just about winning or impressing others. It's about having fun and making memories."

The night of the cultural festival arrived, and the campus was transformed into a vibrant carnival. Stalls offering food from different regions, games, and art exhibitions dotted the grounds. The main stage, where the performances were to take place, was set up with professional sound and lighting, adding to the festive atmosphere.

Euphonic Beats was scheduled to perform in the evening, and as the time approached, Arjun felt a mix of excitement and nervousness. He glanced at his friends, seeing the same emotions reflected in their eyes. "We've got this," he said, trying to boost their confidence. "Let's go out there and give it our all."

Their performance was electrifying. They played a mix of classic rock, contemporary hits, and a few original compositions. The crowd responded enthusiastically, cheering and clapping along with the music. Arjun felt a rush of adrenaline as he played his guitar, the notes flowing effortlessly. The energy of the audience was contagious, and they fed off it, delivering a performance that was both heartfelt and powerful.

As they played their final song, Arjun looked at his friends, feeling a deep sense of pride and gratitude. They had come a long way from their initial rehearsals, and this moment was the culmination of their hard work and dedication. The crowd erupted in applause as they took their final bow, and Arjun knew that this performance would be a cherished memory for years to come.

After their performance, they mingled with the crowd, enjoying the various activities and performances. The festival featured dance performances, theatrical plays, and a fashion show, among other events. The diversity of talent and creativity on display was awe-inspiring, and Arjun felt proud to be a part of such a vibrant community.

One of the highlights of the evening was a dance performance by a group of students who had seamlessly blended traditional Indian dance forms with contemporary styles. The fusion of classical and modern elements created a mesmerizing spectacle that left the audience spellbound.

The fashion show was another major attraction, drawing crowds with its glamorous outfits and confident models. Students from various colleges showcased their designs, ranging from ethnic wear to avant-garde fashion. The energy backstage was palpable, with models making last-minute adjustments and designers giving final touches to their creations.

Kavya, who had a keen interest in fashion, couldn't contain her excitement. "Look at those designs! They're so innovative and bold. I love how they've incorporated traditional elements into modern silhouettes."

Rajat, munching on a samosa, nodded in agreement. "And the confidence of the models! They're owning the runway. It's inspiring to see so much talent."

Suresh, always the tech enthusiast, added, "I loved how they used technology in their performance. The lighting and sound effects added a whole new dimension."

The gaming stalls were another popular spot, drawing large crowds eager to test their skills and win prizes. From traditional games like ring toss and dart throwing to modern video games and VR experiences, there was something for everyone. Arjun and his friends couldn't resist trying their hand at a few games, laughing and cheering each other on.

One of the most memorable moments was when Arjun managed to win a giant teddy bear for Kavya at a ring toss game. The look of surprise and joy on her face was priceless, and it became a symbol of their friendship and the fun they had shared.

The festival also featured various food stalls, offering a wide array of culinary delights. From spicy chaat and crispy dosas to sweet jalebis and creamy kulfi, the aroma of delicious food filled the air. The group indulged in a gastronomic adventure, sampling dishes from different regions and savouring every bite.

As the night wore on, the group found themselves at a food stall, sampling delicious street food and reliving the highlights of the evening. "That dance performance was incredible," Kavya said, savouring a bite of spicy chaat. "The way they fused different styles was so innovative."

Rajat, munching on a samosa, nodded in agreement. "And the energy in their performance was amazing. It's inspiring to see so much talent in one place."

Suresh, always the practical one, said, "And we'll face whatever comes our way, together. We've proven that we can overcome any challenge."

Arjun, feeling a deep sense of gratitude, spoke from the heart. "This festival, this night, it's a reminder of how far we've come and how much we've achieved. But more importantly, it's a celebration of our friendship and the journey we've shared."

They sat by the lake, sharing stories and laughter, until the early hours of the morning. The cultural festival had been more than just an event; it had been a celebration of their journey at NIT, a journey filled with challenges, growth, and unforgettable moments.

As they finally made their way back to their hostel, Arjun felt a sense of fulfilment and happiness. The cultural festival had been a highlight of their college experience, a testament to their hard work, creativity, and the bonds they had formed. It was a night they would remember for the rest of their lives, a night that encapsulated the essence of their time at NIT.

With the memories of the festival fresh in their minds, they returned to their daily routines, ready to tackle the final stretch of their college journey. The cultural festival had recharged their spirits, and they felt more connected and inspired than ever. Arjun knew that whatever challenges lay ahead, they would face them together, as friends and as a team.

The cultural festival had been a celebration of their journey, a reminder of the power of creativity and the importance of community. It had strengthened their resolve and deepened their bonds, preparing them for the final year and the adventures that awaited beyond the gates of NIT.

As the festivities wound down, the students prepared for the next major event on the campus calendar—the Inter-College Sports Extravaganza. With the cultural festival behind them, the focus shifted to athletic competitions, where they would again come together, this time to compete and showcase their sporting talents. The excitement never ceased at NIT, and Arjun and his friends were ready for the next chapter in their incredible journey.

Chapter 16: The Inter-College Sports Extravaganza

The common room was buzzing with excitement as students gathered around the noticeboard. Arjun pushed his way through the crowd to see what the fuss was about. A large poster announced the upcoming Inter-College Sports Extravaganza, where NIT would compete against other engineering colleges in various sports, including badminton and cricket.

Arjun, who had a passion for both badminton and cricket, felt a surge of excitement. This was a chance to represent his college and showcase his skills. He quickly shared the idea with his friends, Rajat, Suresh, and Kavya, who were also eager to participate.

The first step was to join the try-outs for their respective sports. Arjun decided to try out for both the badminton and cricket teams. Rajat opted for football, Suresh for table tennis, and Kavya, who shared Arjun's passion for badminton, also joined the badminton try-outs.

The try-outs were intense, with many talented students competing for spots. Arjun's dedication and skills shone through, earning him places on both the badminton and cricket teams. Kavya also secured a spot on the badminton team, while Rajat and Suresh made it onto their respective teams.

The days leading up to the competition were filled with rigorous training sessions. Early morning runs, practice matches, and team-building exercises became part of their daily routine. The coaches pushed them to their limits, emphasizing the importance of teamwork, strategy, and physical endurance.

As the competition day approached, the campus was electric with anticipation. Students practiced in every corner of the sports complex, and the camaraderie among the athletes was palpable. The shared goal of representing NIT created a strong sense of unity.

Arjun and his friends balanced their academic responsibilities with their training. Despite the exhaustion, they felt more energized and motivated than ever. The support from their peers and the coaching staff kept their spirits high.

Finally, the day of the Inter-College Sports Extravaganza arrived. The campus was decorated with banners and flags, and the stands were filled with cheering students and faculty. The atmosphere was charged with excitement and nervous energy.

The badminton tournament was one of the highlights of the day. Arjun and Kavya, along with their teammates, faced strong competitors from other colleges. The matches were intense, requiring agility, precision, and strategic play.

Arjun's singles match was particularly challenging. His opponent was known for his speed and powerful smashes. Arjun played with a level of focus and intensity he had never experienced before. The cheers from the crowd fuelled his energy as he made precise shots and defended fiercely. The game was neck-and-neck, with the lead constantly changing hands.

In the final moments, Arjun managed a series of well-placed shots that left his opponent scrambling. He secured the winning point with a perfectly timed smash, and the crowd erupted in cheers. Arjun's victory was a significant boost for NIT's standings in the tournament.

Kavya also played exceptionally well in her matches, showcasing her agility and tactical skills. Together, they advanced to the finals in the doubles category, playing a nail-biting match that kept the audience on the edge of their seats. Their teamwork and coordination led them to victory, further solidifying NIT's reputation in badminton.

Meanwhile, Arjun's cricket match was equally thrilling. As an all-rounder, Arjun was crucial to his team's strategy. The match was intense from the start, with both teams displaying excellent skills and tactics.

Arjun's team batted first, setting a challenging target for their opponents. Arjun played a vital role, scoring a half-century with a mix of powerful shots and strategic placements. His performance earned applause from the crowd and boosted his team's morale.

When it was time to bowl, Arjun's precise and aggressive bowling led to key wickets. The match reached a climax in the final overs, with Arjun's team needing to defend a small lead. Arjun bowled the last over, maintaining his composure under pressure and leading his team to a narrow but thrilling victory.

That evening, a grand celebration was held on campus to honour the athletes. The winning teams were awarded trophies and medals, and the atmosphere was filled with joy and pride. Arjun and his friends were congratulated by their peers and professors, their hard work and dedication acknowledged by all.

Arjun felt a deep sense of fulfilment. The experience of competing, pushing his limits, and representing his college was unforgettable. It had taught him valuable lessons about perseverance, teamwork, and the importance of physical fitness.

Back in their hostel room, Arjun and his friends reflected on the incredible journey they had undertaken. They shared stories of their matches, the challenges they had faced, and the exhilaration of their victories.

"This was more than just a sports competition," Rajat said. "It brought us closer as friends and taught us so much about ourselves."

Kavya nodded. "I agree. The discipline and focus we developed during training will definitely help us in our academics and future endeavours."

Arjun smiled, feeling grateful for the experience. "We should continue playing and stay active. It's a great way to balance our studies and keep ourselves motivated."

The Inter-College Sports Extravaganza had been a transformative experience for Arjun and his friends. It reinforced their belief in the importance of a balanced life, where academics and physical activities go hand in hand. With renewed energy and a stronger bond, they looked forward to future challenges, confident in their ability to succeed.

Chapter 17: The Midnight Adventure

It was a typical Wednesday evening when Arjun and his friends stumbled upon a peculiar rumour circulating around campus. Whispered among students and passed down from senior to junior, the tale of a hidden underground floor beneath the old Electrical Engineering building piqued their curiosity. It was said to be a relic from a bygone era, possibly from the time when the college had secret research projects. The underground floor supposedly contained abandoned labs and forgotten experiments.

Arjun, Rajat, Suresh, and Kavya sat in their favourite spot in the common room, discussing the latest assignments and upcoming exams. The conversation took a turn when Rajat mentioned the rumour he had heard from a senior.

"Have you guys heard about the underground floor beneath the Electrical Engineering building?" Rajat asked, his eyes gleaming with excitement.

Suresh raised an eyebrow. "Are you serious? That sounds like something out of a sci-fi movie."

Kavya leaned in, intrigued. "I've heard about it too. Some say it's just a myth, but others swear it's real."

Arjun's curiosity was piqued. "Why don't we check it out? It could be our little adventure. Who knows what we might find?"

The group decided to explore the underground floor that very night. They gathered supplies: flashlights, snacks, and a map of the old Electrical Engineering building that Suresh found online. Excitement mixed with a hint of nervousness as they planned their midnight adventure.

"We should be careful," Kavya cautioned. "We don't know what's down there or if it's even safe."

Arjun nodded. "We'll stick together and turn back if things get too risky."

As the clock struck midnight, the campus grew quiet. The group made their way to the Electrical Engineering building, their hearts pounding with anticipation. The building, shrouded in darkness, looked eerie and imposing. They slipped inside, avoiding the gaze of the night guard.

Using their flashlights, they navigated through dusty corridors and old laboratories. The air was thick with the scent of aged paper and history. They reached the basement, where they believed the entrance to the underground floor was hidden.

Suresh examined the floor and walls, looking for any signs of a hidden passage. After a few minutes, he found a loose tile that, when lifted, revealed a rusted metal handle. With some effort, they managed to pull open a heavy trapdoor, revealing a dark, narrow staircase descending into the depths of the building.

One by one, they climbed down the staircase. The air was cool and damp, and their flashlights cast eerie shadows on the walls. The underground floor was narrow, forcing them to walk in a single file. Despite the cramped space, their excitement kept them moving forward.

They walked for what felt like hours, the tunnel winding and twisting. Occasionally, they found old tools and remnants of past experiments, sparking their imaginations about the underground floor's origins. The atmosphere was tense but exhilarating.

Finally, they reached a heavy metal door with intricate designs. It creaked open, revealing a large underground laboratory. The room was filled with old scientific equipment, dusty computers, and notebooks. The walls were adorned with faded blueprints and technical drawings, hinting at the lab's historical significance.

Kavya picked up an old journal, flipping through its yellowed pages. "This is incredible. It's like stepping into a time capsule."

Suresh examined an ancient blueprint on the wall. "Look at this. It shows experimental designs for early robotics and automation."

Arjun found a cabinet filled with various electronic components and prototypes. "These must be from the early days of electrical engineering research. This place is a treasure trove of history."

As they explored further, they found detailed notes and diagrams about various experiments conducted in the lab. One section of the lab was dedicated to renewable energy projects, with prototypes of solar panels and wind turbines. Another section contained early versions of robotics and automation systems, with half-assembled robots and intricate circuit boards.

"This place is amazing," Rajat said, his voice filled with awe. "These experiments were way ahead of their time."

Kavya nodded, her eyes scanning the room. "It's like these scientists were pioneers. They were working on technology that's only becoming mainstream now."

Suresh, who was particularly fascinated by the robotics section, said, "Imagine what we could learn from their work. This could be valuable for our own projects."

As they marvelled at their discovery, they heard faint footsteps echoing through the underground floor. Their hearts raced as they realized they weren't alone. Panicking, they quickly gathered their things and hid behind a large cabinet.

The footsteps grew louder, and they saw the beam of a flashlight approaching. It was the night guard, likely alerted by the noise they had made. Holding their breaths, they waited until the guard left, barely avoiding being caught.

Once the coast was clear, they carefully retraced their steps, ensuring they left no trace of their presence. Climbing back through the trapdoor, they closed it behind them and made their way out of the building, adrenaline still pumping through their veins.

Back in their hostel room, they shared their findings and celebrated their successful adventure. The experience had brought them closer together, creating memories they would cherish forever.

The next day, they met to discuss what they had found. They decided to document their adventure and the artifacts they had discovered, planning to share it with the Electrical Engineering department. Their midnight adventure had not only been thrilling but had also unearthed a piece of the college's hidden history.

Arjun suggested, "We should create a detailed report and present it to the department head. This discovery could be significant."

Kavya agreed, "And we should include photographs and diagrams of everything we found. It will make our report more credible."

Suresh, ever the tech enthusiast, said, "I'll digitize the blueprints and notes. We can create a digital archive of all the information."

The group spent the next few days compiling their findings. They created a comprehensive report, complete with photographs, diagrams, and detailed descriptions of the experiments and equipment they had discovered. They even included a section on the potential historical significance of the lab and its contributions to modern technology.

When they presented their findings to the head of the Electrical Engineering department, the reaction was one of astonishment and excitement. The department head praised their initiative and thoroughness, promising to investigate further and possibly integrate some of the discovered knowledge into the current curriculum.

Back in their hostel room, Arjun and his friends reflected on the adventure. The bond they shared had grown even stronger through this shared experience.

"This was the most exciting thing we've ever done," Rajat said, grinning from ear to ear.

Arjun nodded, still buzzing with excitement. "We should definitely have more adventures like this. Who knows what other secrets this campus holds?"

Kavya added, "But next time, let's be more careful. We were lucky this time."

Suresh agreed. "Absolutely. But it was worth it. We made history tonight."

The midnight adventure had been a transformative experience for Arjun and his friends. It reinforced their bond and ignited a passion for exploration and discovery. With renewed energy and a stronger sense of friendship, they looked forward to future adventures, confident in their ability to face any challenge together.

Chapter 18: Broken Friendships

Arjun had always valued his friendships deeply. At NIT, his friends were his support system, his partners in crime, and his family away from home. However, as he moved further into his final year, he began to realize that not all friendships were built to withstand the pressures of academic life, personal ambitions, and the inevitable misunderstandings that arose.

The strain on friendships became more apparent during the placement season. The competitive atmosphere at NIT was intense, with everyone vying for the best internships and job offers. Arjun's friend group, which included Rajat, Suresh, and Kavya, had always been tight-knit. They had supported each other through countless late-night study sessions, shared meals, and hostel shenanigans. However, the pressures of securing a future began to take a toll on their camaraderie.

Rajat, who had always been Arjun's closest confidant, started distancing himself. He became increasingly secretive about his plans and seemed more focused on his own goals. Arjun noticed the change but tried to brush it off, attributing it to the stress everyone was under. However, things came to a head when Arjun discovered that Rajat had applied for a highly coveted internship at a top company without informing the rest of the group, despite knowing that Suresh had been eyeing that position for months.

The revelation came during a casual conversation in the common room. Suresh, who had just received a rejection email from the company, was visibly upset. "I can't believe I didn't get it," he muttered. "I thought I had a good chance."

Kavya, trying to comfort Suresh, said, "Maybe they already had someone in mind. You know how these things work."

Arjun, who had been silent, suddenly felt a pang of suspicion. "Rajat, didn't you say you were interested in that position too?" he asked.

Rajat's face flushed. "Uh, yeah, I did. I... I applied too."

The room fell silent. Arjun could feel the tension rising. "You didn't think to mention it to us?" Suresh asked, his voice tinged with betrayal.

Rajat shifted uncomfortably. "I didn't think it was a big deal. We're all applying for different positions, right?"

Suresh stood up, his frustration evident. "It's not about the position, Rajat. It's about trust. We've always been upfront with each other. Why hide it?"

The argument escalated, with harsh words exchanged and old grievances resurfacing. Arjun tried to mediate, but the damage had been done. The fallout left a significant rift in the group, and the once-solid friendship began to crumble.

The emotional impact of the fallout weighed heavily on Arjun. He felt betrayed by Rajat's actions and was hurt by the animosity that had developed among his friends. Nights that were once filled with laughter and camaraderie were now filled with tension and silence. Arjun found himself grappling with feelings of anger, sadness, and confusion. He would lie in bed at night, staring at the ceiling, wondering how things had gone so wrong. The people he had once considered family now felt like strangers.

Determined to find a way forward, Arjun decided to confront Rajat directly. He knew that avoiding the issue would only prolong the pain. One evening, he asked Rajat to meet him by the lake, hoping that the serene environment would facilitate an honest conversation.

As they sat on a bench overlooking the water, Arjun took a deep breath. "Rajat, we need to talk. What happened with the internship really hurt us. Why didn't you tell us?"

Rajat looked down, guilt evident in his eyes. "I didn't mean to hurt anyone, Arjun. I was just so focused on getting the position. I didn't think it would affect our friendship like this."

Arjun nodded, trying to keep his emotions in check. "But it did affect us, Rajat. We've always been honest with each other. This secrecy... it broke our trust."

Rajat sighed. "I know, and I'm sorry. I was scared that if I told you, it would create competition and tension. But I see now that keeping it a secret did more harm than good."

The conversation continued, with both Arjun and Rajat expressing their feelings and grievances. It was a painful but necessary dialogue that allowed them to clear the air. While they didn't resolve everything that night, it was a step towards reconciliation.

In the days that followed, Arjun reached out to Suresh and Kavya, sharing his conversation with Rajat and encouraging them to talk things out. It wasn't easy, but slowly, the group began to heal. They acknowledged their mistakes and made a conscious effort to rebuild their trust and communication.

Despite their efforts, the friendship was never quite the same. The fallout had left scars that couldn't be easily erased. Arjun realized that not all friendships could withstand the test of time and pressure. Some relationships, no matter how strong they seemed, could falter when faced with personal ambitions and misunderstandings.

As he navigated the emotional landscape of broken friendships, Arjun found solace in new connections and rediscovered old ones. He learned to value the friends who stood by him through thick and thin and to let go of those who brought negativity into his life. The experience taught him the importance of resilience, forgiveness, and self-worth.

One afternoon, while studying in the library, Arjun bumped into an old friend from his first year, Neha. They hadn't kept in touch much, but seeing a familiar face brought a sense of comfort. They decided to grab a coffee and catch up.

Over steaming cups of tea, Arjun shared his recent struggles. Neha listened attentively, offering words of support and wisdom. "Friendships can be complicated, Arjun," she said. "But remember, it's the genuine connections that matter. Sometimes, letting go is necessary for personal growth."

Her words resonated with Arjun. He realized that his journey at NIT was about more than just academics and achievements. It was about the relationships he built and the lessons he learned along the way.

Neha's encouragement gave Arjun the strength to face the reality of his fractured friendships. He decided to reach out to Suresh and Kavya individually, hoping to mend the rifts that had formed.

First, he met Suresh in the canteen, choosing a quiet corner where they could talk without interruptions. Suresh was hesitant at first, but as Arjun opened up about his feelings of betrayal and hurt, Suresh began to soften.

"I never meant for things to get this bad," Suresh admitted, his voice tinged with regret. "I was just so angry and felt like everything was falling apart."

Arjun nodded, understanding the emotions that had fuelled their conflict. "I know, Suresh. We've all been under a lot of stress. But our friendship is important to me, and I don't want it to end like this."

They talked for hours, airing out their grievances and sharing their perspectives. By the end of the conversation, they had reached a tentative truce, agreeing to work on rebuilding their trust.

Next, Arjun approached Kavya. She had always been the peacekeeper in their group, and her absence during the fallout had been particularly painful. They met in the campus garden, surrounded by the calming presence of nature.

"Kavya, I miss our friendship," Arjun began, his voice filled with emotion. "I know things have been tough, but I believe we can get through this together."

Kavya's eyes welled up with tears. "I miss you too, Arjun. It's been hard seeing our group fall apart. But I'm willing to try and fix things if you are."

With heartfelt conversations and mutual understanding, Arjun and Kavya began to heal their fractured friendship. They promised to be more open and honest with each other, recognizing the importance of communication in maintaining strong relationships.

Despite these efforts, Rajat remained distant. Arjun couldn't shake the feeling that their friendship had suffered irreparable damage. He decided to give Rajat some space, hoping that time would heal the wounds and allow them to find common ground once again.

As the semester progressed, Arjun focused on his studies and extracurricular activities, finding solace in the routine and the support of his friends. He continued to nurture his relationships with Suresh and Kavya, appreciating the renewed sense of camaraderie and trust.

One evening, as Arjun was working late in the library, he received a message from Rajat. It was a simple text, asking if they could meet and talk. Arjun's heart raced as he read the message, feeling a mixture of hope and apprehension.

They met at the same bench by the lake where they had once shared so many conversations. Rajat looked nervous, but there was a determination in his eyes that Arjun hadn't seen in a long time.

Arjun, I've had a lot of time to think," Rajat began, his voice steady. "I realize now how much I've hurt you and the group. I let my ambitions get in the way of our friendship, and I'm truly sorry."

Arjun felt a surge of emotion, his anger and hurt melting away in the face of Rajat's sincerity. "Rajat, I appreciate you saying that. Our friendship means a lot to me, and I want to move past this. But it's going to take time to rebuild the trust."

Rajat nodded, understanding the gravity of Arjun's words. "I know, and I'm willing to put in the effort. I miss the way things used to be, and I want to make things right."

Their conversation continued late into the night, filled with apologies, reflections, and hopes for the future. It wasn't an instant fix, but it was a step in the right direction. Arjun felt a sense of relief, knowing that the path to healing had begun.

As the days turned into weeks, Arjun and Rajat slowly mended their friendship. They worked on being more open and honest with each other, recognizing the importance of trust and communication. The process was gradual, but with each passing day, their bond grew stronger.

Arjun found himself reflecting on his time at NIT. The experiences, both good and bad, had shaped him into a stronger, more self-aware individual. He had faced the highs and lows of friendships, navigated the complexities of love, and emerged with a deeper understanding of himself and his values.

With their friendship on the mend, Arjun and Rajat, along with their group of friends, decided to focus on making the most of their remaining time at NIT. They joined new clubs, took on leadership roles in student organizations, and participated in various campus events. These activities not only enriched their college experience but also strengthened their bond as friends.

One weekend, the group planned a hiking trip to a nearby hill station. It was a refreshing break from their academic pressures, and they spent the days exploring trails, sharing stories around the campfire, and enjoying the natural beauty. The trip brought them closer together, reinforcing the importance of taking time to relax and connect with each other.

Back on campus, they decided to start a community service initiative. Inspired by the needs they saw around them, they began organizing weekly visits to a local orphanage. They helped the children with their studies, organized games, and conducted workshops to teach them new skills. This experience was profoundly impactful for Arjun, as it allowed him to see beyond the college bubble and contribute to the community.

The group's efforts were recognized by the college administration, and they were given a small grant to expand their activities. They used the funds to set up a library at the orphanage, stocked with books and learning materials. The joy on the children's faces when the library was unveiled was one of the most rewarding moments for Arjun and his friends.

Amidst these activities, Arjun continued to excel academically, finding a balance between his studies and extracurricular pursuits. He discovered a passion for research and started working on a project with one of his professors, delving into innovative solutions for real-world problems. The project was challenging but rewarding, and it opened his eyes to new possibilities for his future career.

Arjun also found time to mentor junior students, sharing his experiences and offering guidance to help them navigate the challenges of college life. His journey at NIT had taught him the value of community and support, and he wanted to give back by helping others.

As the semester progressed, Arjun and his friends faced various ups and downs, but they faced them together, their friendship growing stronger with each challenge. They learned to rely on each other, to celebrate each other's successes, and to provide comfort during difficult times.

With each passing day, Arjun felt more confident and prepared for the future. He knew that his time at NIT was not just about academic achievements but also about the relationships and experiences that had shaped him. The journey was ongoing, and he was ready to embrace whatever came next, knowing that he had the support of his friends and the skills he had developed.

And so, Arjun's story continued, filled with new adventures, personal growth, and the certainty that he would face whatever came his way with strength and courage. The world awaited, and Arjun was ready to make his mark, one step at a time.

Chapter 19: The Research Project

Arjun's final year at NIT was in full swing, and he found himself immersed in a new challenge: the mandatory research project. Each student was required to work on a project that would not only test their technical skills but also their ability to innovate and solve real-world problems. Arjun was both excited and nervous as he began this new journey.

His project focused on renewable energy solutions, specifically on improving the efficiency of solar panels. Arjun had always been passionate about sustainable energy, and this project was the perfect opportunity to delve deeper into the field. He teamed up with his friends Kavya and Suresh, whose expertise complemented his own.

The initial weeks were spent in the library and laboratories, gathering data, reading research papers, and brainstorming ideas. They faced numerous challenges, from technical glitches to theoretical roadblocks, but their determination kept them going. They also sought guidance from Dr. Menon, a professor known for his expertise in renewable energy.

One afternoon, as they were huddled around a table in the lab, Dr. Menon walked in. "How's the project coming along?" he asked, peering over Arjun's shoulder at the array of data spread out before them.

"We're making progress, sir, but we're struggling with the efficiency calculations," Arjun admitted.

Dr. Menon nodded thoughtfully. "The key is to think outside the box. Sometimes, the solution isn't in the data but in how you interpret it. Have you considered looking into advanced materials or different angles for panel placement?"

This advice sparked a new wave of ideas. They decided to experiment with various materials and configurations, even staying late into the night to test their hypotheses. The camaraderie among the team grew stronger as they worked tirelessly, their shared goal fostering a sense of unity and purpose.

One night, after a particularly successful experiment, they sat on the rooftop of the hostel, overlooking the quiet campus. "Can you believe we actually got it to work?" Kavya said, her eyes shining with excitement.

Arjun smiled, feeling a sense of accomplishment. "It's amazing what we can achieve when we work together. This project is more than just a grade; it's about making a real impact."

As the deadline for the project submission approached, the pressure intensified. Arjun, Kavya, and Suresh spent countless hours in the lab, fine-tuning their research and experiments, ensuring every detail was perfect. The journey towards completing their project on improving the efficiency of solar panels began with a series of brainstorming sessions. They considered various materials, innovative configurations, and cutting-edge technologies.

"We need to look at this problem from multiple angles," Suresh suggested during one late-night session in the library. "What if we explore nanomaterials? They have the potential to significantly enhance the absorption of sunlight."

Kavya nodded, her eyes lighting up with enthusiasm. "That's a great idea, Suresh. Nanomaterials can increase the surface area and improve the efficiency of light capture. We should definitely include this in our research."

Arjun added, "We should also experiment with different angles for panel placement. The conventional flat panels might not be the most efficient. Tilting them or using tracking systems to follow the sun could yield better results."

With these ideas in mind, they divided the tasks among themselves. Kavya would focus on researching nanomaterials and their applications in solar panels, Suresh would handle the technical aspects of panel configurations and tracking systems, and Arjun would coordinate the project, ensuring that all parts came together seamlessly.

Days turned into weeks as they delved deeper into their research. The lab became their second home, filled with the hum of equipment and the smell of chemicals. They faced numerous setbacks, from malfunctioning equipment to inconclusive results, but each challenge only strengthened their resolve.

One particularly frustrating evening, they encountered a major roadblock. The efficiency of the solar panels was not improving despite their best efforts. They sat in the lab, exhausted and disheartened.

"This isn't working," Kavya said, her voice tinged with frustration. "We've tried everything, but the efficiency just isn't where it needs to be."

Arjun, trying to remain positive, suggested, "Maybe we need to take a step back and re-evaluate our approach. Let's look at the data again and see if there's something we've missed."

They spent the next few hours poring over their data, analyzing every detail. As the night wore on, a pattern began to emerge. They realized that the issue was not with the materials or the configurations, but with the integration of the two.

"We need to ensure that the nanomaterials and the tracking systems are working in harmony," Suresh said, excitement returning to his voice. "If we can synchronize them better, we might see the improvements we're looking for."

With renewed energy, they went back to the lab, adjusting their experiments to better integrate the nanomaterials and tracking systems. This time, their efforts paid off. The efficiency of the solar panels began to show significant improvement.

Their breakthrough was a turning point. The excitement in the lab was palpable as they ran test after test, each one confirming their findings. They had done it – they had found a way to significantly improve the efficiency of solar panels.

The night before their final presentation, the team decided to take a break and relax on the rooftop of their hostel. The campus was quiet, the air cool and refreshing. They sat together, looking out over the sprawling grounds of NIT, feeling a deep sense of satisfaction.

"It's hard to believe how far we've come," Kavya said, breaking the silence. "From those initial brainstorming sessions to actually achieving our goals."

Arjun smiled, feeling a sense of camaraderie with his friends. "We've worked so hard, and it's paid off. This project is proof that we can overcome any challenge if we stick together."

Suresh raised an imaginary glass. "To teamwork, perseverance, and making a real impact."

The day of the presentation arrived, and they stood nervously outside the lecture hall, waiting for their turn. The hall was filled with professors, industry experts, and fellow students, all eager to see the results of their hard work.

As they stepped onto the stage, Arjun took a deep breath and began. He outlined their journey, from the initial ideas to the challenges they faced and the innovative solutions they developed. Kavya and Suresh followed, explaining the technical aspects and the potential real-world applications of their research.

When they finished, the room was silent for a moment before erupting in applause. Dr. Menon stood up, a proud smile on his face. "Excellent work, all of you. This is precisely the kind of innovation and dedication we strive to cultivate here at NIT."

The project was a resounding success, earning them top marks and recognition within the academic community. More importantly, it solidified Arjun's belief in his abilities and the power of teamwork. This experience was a testament to their hard work, resilience, and the bonds they had formed over the years.

As they celebrated their success, Arjun reflected on his journey. From a hesitant first-year student to a confident final-year researcher, he had come a long way. The challenges, the friendships, and the experiences had shaped him into a well-rounded individual ready to take on the world.

The research project was not just an academic requirement; it was a pivotal moment in Arjun's life, demonstrating the power of perseverance and collaboration. The lessons learned and the memories made during this journey would stay with him forever, guiding him in his future endeavours.

Chapter 20: Placement Preparations

After the success of his research project, Arjun approached the new semester at NIT with a renewed sense of confidence and purpose. The accolades and recognition he had received for his work had been a significant boost, further solidifying his determination to excel. As the semester began, the buzz around campus was palpable – placement season was approaching, and the pressure to secure a job was mounting.

The rigorous preparation for campus placements began in earnest. Arjun knew that a strong resume was crucial, so he meticulously updated it, highlighting his academic achievements, extracurricular activities, and the practical experience he had gained during his internship. He spent countless hours refining his resume, ensuring that it showcased his strengths and potential.

In addition to building his resume, Arjun attended various workshops and seminars organized by the placement cell. These sessions covered a range of topics, from resume writing and interview techniques to group discussions and aptitude tests. Arjun immersed himself in these activities, determined to leave no stone unturned in his preparation.

One of the most challenging aspects of the preparation was practicing for interviews. Arjun and his friends formed a study group, conducting mock interviews and providing each other with constructive feedback. They simulated real interview scenarios, asking tough questions and pushing each other to think critically and articulate their thoughts clearly.

"Arjun, tell me about a time when you faced a significant challenge and how you overcame it," Suresh asked during one of their mock interviews.

Arjun took a deep breath, recalling his experience during the internship reorganization. "During my internship, I was reassigned to a new project mid-way, which involved working on a complex software system. Initially, I struggled to adapt, but I sought guidance from my teammates and focused on building relationships. By the end of the project, I had successfully contributed to a critical task and gained valuable insights into the new domain."

The mock interviews were intense, but they helped Arjun build confidence and refine his responses. The support and camaraderie of his friends provided a sense of reassurance and motivation.

As the placement season approached, the anticipation and anxiety among students reached a fever pitch. The pressure to secure a job, coupled with the fear of rejection, created a charged atmosphere on campus. Arjun, despite his strong profile, was not immune to these feelings.

The first round of placements began, and Arjun faced his initial interviews with a mix of excitement and nerves. However, despite his thorough preparation, he faced a series of rejections. Each rejection chipped away at his confidence.

One evening, after receiving yet another rejection email, Arjun sat in his room, feeling defeated. "Why is this happening? I've worked so hard, and I have a strong profile. What am I doing wrong?" he wondered aloud.

Kavya, who had been a constant source of support, tried to console him. "Arjun, sometimes it's not about your qualifications or your performance. There are so many factors at play. Don't lose hope. Keep pushing forward."

The rejections took a toll on Arjun's mental health. He found it difficult to focus on his studies, and the stress began to manifest physically. He struggled with sleepless nights and a lack of appetite, feeling overwhelmed by the pressure and disappointment.

In the midst of this turmoil, Arjun decided to seek help from the campus counselling centre again. The counsellor provided a safe space for Arjun to express his feelings and fears. Through their sessions, Arjun began to understand the importance of mental health and self-care.

"Arjun, it's crucial to take care of yourself during this challenging time," the counsellor advised. "Focus on the things you can control, and be kind to yourself. Rejections are a part of life, but they don't define your worth."

With the counsellor's guidance, Arjun started incorporating self-care practices into his routine. He made time for exercise, meditation, and activities that brought him joy, such as playing cricket and listening to music. Slowly, he began to rebuild his confidence and regain a sense of balance.

Despite his efforts to maintain a balanced routine, Arjun often found himself awake in the middle of the night, his mind racing with worries and fears about his academic performance and placement prospects. The pressure to excel, coupled with the fear of failure, created a constant state of anxiety that left him feeling drained and exhausted.

One particularly difficult night, Arjun decided to take a walk around the campus to clear his mind. The cool night air provided a temporary respite from the suffocating pressure he felt. As he wandered aimlessly, he stumbled upon a bench near the serene campus lake. He sat down, the silence of the night amplifying the thoughts swirling in his mind.

"Why am I struggling so much?" Arjun thought to himself, frustration evident in his expression. "I used to be so confident, so sure of myself. What changed?"

The reflection on his struggles brought a flood of emotions. Arjun felt tears welling up in his eyes as he grappled with the weight of his expectations and the fear of letting himself and his family down. The tears flowed freely, a cathartic release of the pent-up stress and anxiety he had been carrying.

In that moment of vulnerability, Arjun realized the importance of self-compassion. He had been so focused on achieving perfection that he had forgotten to acknowledge his own humanity. The setback he faced was not a reflection of his worth, but rather an opportunity for growth and learning.

As the first half of the placement season came to a close, Arjun decided to take a short break to visit his family. The time away from campus provided a much-needed respite and an opportunity to recharge. His family's unwavering support and encouragement reminded him of his strengths and potential.

Returning to campus with a renewed sense of determination, Arjun set his sights on the second half of the placement season. He approached each interview with a fresh perspective, focusing on presenting his true self and showcasing his resilience.

One evening, as Arjun was preparing for an interview with Rockwell Corporation, a leading finance company, he received an unexpected message from Neha. "Arjun, I know things have been tough, and I hope you're doing well. Remember, your hard work will pay off."

The message stirred a mix of emotions within Arjun, but it also served as a reminder of how far he had come. He realized that his journey was about more than just securing a job; it was about personal growth and resilience.

The interview with Rockwell Corporation was intense, but Arjun felt a sense of calm and confidence as he answered their questions. He spoke passionately about his experiences, his learnings, and his aspirations.

A few days later, Arjun received a call from Rockwell Corporation with an offer. He had secured a position with the highest package in his batch. The sense of accomplishment was overwhelming, and tears of joy streamed down his face.

"Guys, I got the job!" Arjun announced to his friends, his voice choked with emotion.

Suresh, Kavya, and Rajat erupted in cheers, enveloping him in a group hug. "You did it, Arjun! We knew you would!"

The journey had been challenging, filled with setbacks and emotional turmoil, but the reward was worth the struggle. Arjun's success taught him the importance of patience, resilience, and mental health.

As he stood on the threshold of a new chapter, Arjun felt a profound sense of gratitude and accomplishment. The trials and tribulations he had faced had shaped him into a stronger, more self-aware individual.

Chapter 21: The Final Year

The final year at NIT brought a mix of emotions for Arjun Mehra. With his placement at Rockwell Corporation secured, a sense of relief and accomplishment washed over him. Yet, the realization that his time in college was coming to an end filled him with a bittersweet feeling. The campus that had been his home for the past few years, the friends who had become his family, and the experiences that had shaped him were now precious memories he would soon leave behind.

As the academic year progressed, Arjun found himself reflecting on his journey. From the initial days of culture shock and homesickness to the highs and lows of academic pressures, friendships, and relationships, every moment had contributed to his personal growth. He had transformed from a pampered boy into a resilient and self-aware young man, ready to take on the world.

One crisp morning, as Arjun sat by the campus lake with Kavya, Suresh, and Rajat, they reminisced about their time at NIT. The serene water mirrored the sky, creating a peaceful backdrop for their conversation.

"Remember our first year?" Suresh said, chuckling. "We were so clueless about everything. And look at us now, all set to graduate."

Kavya nodded, her eyes misty with nostalgia. "We've come a long way. The late-night study sessions, the club activities, the trips – it's all been so memorable."

Rajat leaned back, looking at the sky. "I'm going to miss this place. We've made so many memories here."

Arjun smiled, feeling a pang of sadness. "Yeah, it's been an incredible journey. But we still have a few months left. Let's make the most of it."

Determined to create lasting memories, Arjun and his friends planned several trips and activities. They visited nearby hill stations, explored the city's hidden gems, and even took a spontaneous road trip to a coastal town. Each trip was filled with laughter, adventure, and bonding, strengthening their friendships even further.

One weekend, they decided to visit the nearby hill station of Manali. The winding roads, the lush greenery, and the cool mountain air provided a refreshing change from their routine. They spent their days trekking, exploring local markets, and enjoying the breath-taking views. The evenings were filled with bonfires, music, and deep conversations under the starry sky.

On the last night of their trip, they sat around the bonfire, sharing their hopes and dreams for the future. Arjun spoke about his excitement for his new job at Rockwell Corporation, but also confessed his fears about leaving the familiar environment of NIT.

"It's scary, you know?" Arjun said, staring into the flames. "The thought of starting a new chapter, away from all of you, in a completely different environment. I hope I can handle it."

Kavya placed a reassuring hand on his shoulder. "Arjun, you've faced so many challenges and come out stronger every time. You'll do great. And we'll always be here for you, no matter where life takes us."

Suresh nodded in agreement. "Yeah, we'll stay in touch. And who knows, maybe we'll all end up in the same city someday."

Rajat grinned. "Or we can plan more trips like this one. Distance won't change our friendship."

The warmth of their words and the camaraderie they shared filled Arjun with a sense of comfort. The future was uncertain, but with friends like these, he felt ready to face whatever came his way.

Back on campus, the final semester was a whirlwind of activities. Arjun balanced his academic responsibilities with the desire to spend quality time with his friends. They attended campus events, participated in farewell parties, and captured countless memories in photos and videos.

The final exams approached, bringing with them a mix of stress and anticipation. Arjun spent long hours in the library, revising his notes and preparing for the last set of exams he would take as a student. The realization that this chapter of his life was coming to an end made him appreciate each moment even more.

One evening, as Arjun sat in his dorm room surrounded by textbooks and notes, he took a moment to look around. The walls were adorned with posters and photographs that captured the essence of his college journey. Each picture told a story – late-night study sessions, festival celebrations, spontaneous trips, and cherished moments with friends.

A knock on the door interrupted his thoughts. It was Suresh, holding a tray with cups of tea.

"Thought you could use a break," Suresh said, handing Arjun a cup.

Arjun smiled gratefully. "Thanks, man. I was just thinking about how much I'm going to miss all of this."

Suresh sat down, his expression thoughtful. "Yeah, it's hard to believe it's almost over. But think of it this way – we've made memories that will last a lifetime. And we'll carry these experiences with us, no matter where we go."

Arjun nodded, taking a sip of the warm tea. "You're right. It's been an incredible journey. And I wouldn't trade it for anything."

As the final exams loomed, Arjun and his friends found themselves entrenched in their studies. Days were spent in the library, hunched over textbooks and notes, while nights turned into marathon revision sessions. The campus buzzed with a mixture of anxiety and determination as students pushed their limits. Arjun could feel the weight of the pressure bearing down on him, but the camaraderie with his friends was a source of comfort. They motivated each other through moments of doubt, offering words of encouragement and celebrating small victories, like mastering a particularly tough concept or completing a challenging practice exam.

The night before the first exam, the group gathered in their usual study spot, the air thick with nervous energy. "We've got this," Suresh said, his voice steady. "We've prepared well. Let's just do our best." They all nodded in agreement, drawing strength from each other's resolve.

When exam day finally arrived, the atmosphere on campus was electric. Arjun walked into the exam hall with a sense of calm determination, a stark contrast to the chaos of his mind. He took a deep breath and focused on the task at hand, methodically working through each question. The hours seemed to stretch endlessly, but when he finally put down his pen, a wave of relief washed over him.

After the last exam, the entire campus seemed to breathe a collective sigh of relief. The sense of achievement was palpable, but it was mixed with a growing excitement for what lay ahead. Arjun and his friends decided to celebrate their hard work with a much-deserved break. They planned a trip to a nearby hill station, a place known for its serene landscapes and tranquil environment.

The trip was exactly what they needed. As they hiked through lush trails, shared stories around a campfire, and gazed at the starry night sky, they felt the stress of the exams melt away. The days were filled with laughter and relaxation, and the nights with deep conversations about their dreams and aspirations.

One evening, while sitting on a cliff overlooking the valley, Kavya broke the comfortable silence. "This place is magical. It's like we're suspended between the past and the future, just for a little while."

Rajat nodded. "Yeah, it's the perfect way to transition from one phase of our lives to the next."

Suresh looked thoughtful. "You know, we've always talked about our professional goals, but what about personal ones? What kind of people do we want to be?"

Arjun smiled, appreciating the shift in the conversation. "I want to be someone who makes a positive impact, not just through my work, but in how I treat others. I want to be remembered for my kindness and integrity."

Kavya agreed. "I want to continue volunteering, helping those in need. It's something that has always given me a sense of purpose."

Rajat added, "I want to travel more, to understand different cultures and perspectives. It broadens the mind and the heart."

Suresh raised his glass. "To becoming the best versions of ourselves, both professionally and personally."

"To that," Arjun echoed, raising his own glass. They clinked their glasses together, sealing their unspoken promises.

As they returned to campus, refreshed and recharged, they found themselves more connected than ever. They spent their remaining days at NIT enjoying the simple pleasures of student life—late-night discussions, spontaneous outings, and making the most of their time together.

One memorable day, they decided to visit the local orphanage where they had volunteered during their college years. The children greeted them with excitement, and the visit turned into a joyful reunion. Seeing the smiles on the children's faces, Arjun felt a deep sense of fulfilment, realizing the positive impact they had made.

As they left the orphanage, Kavya turned to Arjun. "These moments remind us of the difference we can make. No matter where we go, let's carry this spirit with us."

Arjun nodded, feeling a sense of purpose. "Absolutely. It's not just about what we achieve professionally; it's also about the positive impact we can have on others."

As the days passed, the reality of their impending separation began to sink in. Arjun and his friends faced the inevitable goodbyes with a mix of sadness and determination. They promised to stay in touch, to support each other through the ups and downs, and to reunite whenever possible.

On their last night together, they gathered in Arjun's room for one final celebration. They laughed, reminisced, and shared their dreams for the future. The room was filled with a bittersweet sense of closure and new beginnings.

Arjun stood up, holding his glass. "To us, and to the journey ahead. No matter where life takes us, we'll always have these memories and this bond. Thank you for being a part of my life."

The room erupted in cheers, and they clinked their glasses one last time. The night was filled with heartfelt toasts, tearful farewells, and the promise of enduring friendship.

As Arjun packed his belongings the next day, he felt a mix of emotions. The familiar surroundings of his dorm room, the laughter and camaraderie of his friends, and the memories of his college years all tugged at his heart. But beneath the nostalgia was a sense of excitement and anticipation for the future.

With his bags packed and his room empty, Arjun took one last look around. He closed the door behind him, carrying with him the lessons, memories, and friendships that had defined his time at NIT.

As he stepped out into the world beyond, Arjun felt a surge of confidence. Though the path ahead was filled with unknowns, he embraced the thrill of discovery and the promise of new beginnings, ready to meet every challenge with strong determination.

Chapter 22: Graduation and Beyond

Graduation day dawned bright and clear, a stark contrast to the storm of emotions brewing within Arjun. As he donned his graduation robe and adjusted his cap, he couldn't help but reflect on the journey that had brought him to this moment. The past few years at NIT had been filled with growth, challenges, and unforgettable memories, and now it was time to say goodbye.

The campus was abuzz with excitement, families bustling around to capture every moment, and students exchanging nervous smiles. Arjun's parents had travelled to attend the ceremony, their faces beaming with pride. As he joined his friends, he felt a lump in his throat. The day was a celebration of their achievements, but it also marked the end of an era.

The graduation ceremony was a blur of speeches, applause, and the procession of graduates receiving their degrees. When Arjun's name was called, he walked across the stage with a mix of pride and melancholy. As he shook hands with the dean and accepted his degree, the weight of the moment settled in. This was the culmination of years of hard work, late-night study sessions, and personal growth.

After the ceremony, Arjun and his friends gathered with their families for photographs. The campus, which had been their home for so long, now served as the backdrop for their final moments together as students.

"Can you believe it's over?" Kavya asked, her voice tinged with sadness.

"It's hard to wrap my head around," Suresh replied. "We've been through so much together."

Arjun nodded, looking around at his friends. "This place has shaped us in ways we can't even begin to understand. But now, it's time for the next chapter."

As the evening wore on, the celebrations continued with a grand graduation party. The air was filled with laughter, music, and the bittersweet joy of shared memories. Arjun and his friends danced, toasted to their future, and reminisced about their time at NIT. The bonds they had formed felt unbreakable, and the promise of staying connected provided a sense of comfort.

The next morning, reality began to set in. Arjun had secured a job at Rockwell Corporation, and the transition from student to professional life loomed ahead. The excitement of starting a new chapter was mixed with the anxiety of leaving the familiar behind. Arjun's family was supportive, but the thought of moving to a new city and adapting to a professional environment felt daunting.

With the departure day approaching, Arjun decided to take a final stroll around the campus. Each corner held memories—lecture halls where he had spent countless hours, the library that was almost a second home, and the canteen where laughter echoed during meal breaks. He visited the dormitory roof, where he and his friends often gathered to unwind and gaze at the stars, reflecting on their dreams and aspirations.

As he walked, Arjun bumped into familiar faces—professors who had mentored him, juniors who looked up to him, and friends who shared his journey. Each encounter was filled with heartfelt exchanges and best wishes for the future. The campus, which had been bustling with activity, now felt like a cherished scrapbook of memories.

The day of departure arrived, and Arjun's friends gathered to bid him farewell. The goodbyes were filled with hugs, tears, and promises to stay in touch. Suresh, Kavya, and Rajat stood with him at the campus gate, the place where their journey had begun.

"We'll miss you, Arjun," Kavya said, her voice trembling. "But we know you'll do great things."

"Keep in touch, man," Suresh added, trying to keep his emotions in check. "We'll visit you whenever we can."

Rajat gave Arjun a tight hug. "You've got this, Arjun. And remember, we're always here for you."

Arjun felt a surge of gratitude for his friends. They had been his support system through thick and thin, and their words gave him the strength to face the unknown. As he boarded the train, he looked back at the campus one last time, a place that had given him so much.

The journey to the new city was filled with mixed emotions. Arjun stared out the window, the landscape changing as he moved further away from the familiarity of NIT. The excitement of starting a new job was tinged with the sadness of leaving his friends and the comfort of college life.

Arriving in the bustling city, Arjun felt a sense of disorientation. The towering buildings and busy streets were a stark contrast to the serene campus he had left behind. Finding his apartment and settling in was a challenge, but Arjun was determined to adapt. The first few days were a whirlwind of unpacking, exploring the city, and preparing for his new job.

The first day at Rockwell Corporation was both exhilarating and nerve-wracking. The professional environment was vastly different from the academic world Arjun was accustomed to. He was introduced to his team, and his mentor, Mr. Patel, provided a warm welcome.

"Welcome to Rockwell, Arjun," Mr. Patel said with a smile. "We're excited to have you on board. You'll find that the transition from college to the professional world can be challenging, but also very rewarding."

Arjun nodded, feeling a mix of excitement and nervousness. "Thank you, Mr. Patel. I'm looking forward to learning and contributing."

The initial days were filled with orientation sessions, meetings, and getting acquainted with the company's projects and processes. Arjun faced a steep learning curve, but his experiences at NIT had equipped him with the resilience and adaptability needed to navigate the challenges. He found himself drawing on the skills he had developed during his internship and the lessons he had learned from his professors and friends.

Despite the busy schedule, Arjun made time to stay connected with his friends from NIT. They had created a group chat to share updates, support each other, and reminisce about their college days. The messages were a lifeline, providing a sense of continuity and reminding Arjun that he was not alone in this new phase of life.

As weeks turned into months, Arjun began to find his footing at Rockwell Corporation. The initial nerves gave way to confidence as he took on more responsibilities and contributed to significant projects. His team members were supportive, and Mr. Patel's mentorship proved invaluable.

One evening, after a particularly productive day at work, Arjun sat in his apartment reflecting on his journey. The transition had been challenging, but he felt a deep sense of fulfilment. The experiences at NIT had prepared him for this moment, and he realized the importance of everything he had learned.

The lessons of perseverance, teamwork, and adaptability were now guiding him in the professional world. The friendships he had formed provided a source of strength and support, even from a distance. The challenges he had faced had shaped him into a resilient individual, ready to tackle whatever came his way.

As Arjun settled into his routine, he also made an effort to explore the new city. He visited cultural landmarks, tried different cuisines, and attended local events. Each experience added a new dimension to his life, broadening his perspective and helping him grow.

One weekend, Arjun decided to take a solo trip to a nearby hill station. The mountains, with their serene beauty and fresh air, reminded him of the trips he had taken with his friends. As he trekked through the trails, he felt a sense of peace and clarity. The journey had been long and winding, but each step had brought him closer to understanding himself and his path.

Sitting on a rock, overlooking a breath-taking valley, Arjun took out his phone and called Kavya. The familiar voice on the other end brought a smile to his face.

"Hey Kavya, guess where I am?" Arjun said, his voice filled with excitement.

"Arjun! Where are you?" Kavya's voice was equally enthusiastic.

"I'm at a hill station, just like the trips we used to take. It's beautiful here, and it made me think of all the adventures we had."

Kavya laughed. "That sounds amazing. We miss you, Arjun. When are you coming back to visit?"

"Soon, hopefully," Arjun replied, feeling a pang of longing. "We need to plan a reunion. It's not the same without you guys."

As they chatted, Arjun felt a renewed sense of connection. The distance had not diminished their bond, and the memories they had created continued to be a source of joy and strength.

Returning to the city, Arjun felt reinvigorated. The trip had given him the perspective he needed to embrace the present and look forward to the future. He realized that while the journey had its ups and downs, each experience was a stepping stone to personal and professional growth.

As the year progressed, Arjun continued to excel at Rockwell Corporation. He received recognition for his contributions and was given opportunities to lead projects and mentor new hires. The challenges he had faced, both at NIT and in his early days at the company, had prepared him well.

One evening, as Arjun walked home from work, he received a call from Mr. Patel. "Arjun, I wanted to let you know that you've been selected for a special project. It's a great opportunity, and we believe you're the right person for the job."

Arjun felt a surge of pride and excitement. "Thank you, Mr. Patel. I'm honoured and ready to take on the challenge."

As he hung up, Arjun couldn't help but reflect on the journey that had brought him here. The experiences at NIT, the support of his friends and mentors, and the challenges he had overcome had all contributed to his growth and success.

That night, Arjun sat by his window, looking out at the city lights. The future was still uncertain, but he felt a deep sense of gratitude for the journey so far. The lessons, friendships, and experiences from NIT had shaped him into the person he was today, and he knew they would continue to guide him in the years to come.

As the months passed, Arjun found himself fully immersed in his role at Rockwell Corporation. His hard work and dedication paid off, and he began to make a name for himself within the company. However, the busy professional life did not come without its own set of challenges.

One evening, Arjun received a message from Anuska, his ex-girlfriend from his first year at NIT. It had been a long time since they had spoken, and seeing her name brought back a flood of memories.

"Hey Arjun, I heard about your success at Rockwell. I'm proud of what you've become. Would love to catch up if you're free sometime."

Arjun felt a mix of emotions as he read the message. Anuska had been an important part of his life, and though their relationship had ended, he had always wished her well. He decided to meet her, curious to see how she was doing and to share their journeys since they had last met.

They met at a cosy café in the city. Anuska looked radiant, and as they exchanged pleasantries, it was clear that both of them had grown and matured over the years.

"It's so good to see you, Arjun," Anuska said with a warm smile. "I've been following your achievements, and I must say, I'm really proud of you."

Arjun smiled, feeling a sense of gratitude. "Thank you, Anuska. It means a lot. How have you been?"

They spent the evening catching up, sharing their experiences and reflecting on their college days. The conversation flowed easily, and by the end of the evening, they parted on good terms, happy to have reconnected.

A few weeks later, Arjun ran into Neha, another significant person from his past, at a networking event. Neha had been a close friend and a source of emotional support during some of his toughest times at NIT. Seeing her brought a smile to his face.

"Neha! It's been ages. How have you been?" Arjun exclaimed, giving her a warm hug.

"Arjun! I've been good. And I've been hearing great things about you. Rockwell Corporation, huh? That's impressive!" Neha replied, her eyes sparkling with excitement.

They found a quiet corner to chat, reminiscing about their college days and sharing their current experiences. Neha's enthusiasm and positivity were infectious, and Arjun felt a renewed sense of connection with his past.

"Arjun, you've come such a long way. I'm so proud of you," Neha said, her voice filled with genuine admiration.

"Thank you, Neha. Your support meant a lot to me back then. It's great to see you doing well too," Arjun replied, feeling a deep sense of gratitude for the people who had been part of his journey.

As Arjun continued to navigate his professional life, these reconnections served as reminders of his growth and the importance of the relationships he had built over the years. Each encounter reinforced the value of his experiences at NIT and the people who had shaped his journey.

The challenges of the professional world were real, but Arjun faced them with the resilience and determination he had developed over the years. The lessons from NIT, the support of his friends and mentors, and the experiences that had shaped him provided a solid foundation for his future endeavours.

Epilogue: A New Chapter Begins

Arjun Mehra sat by the window of his apartment, the city lights twinkling below. The journey from his pampered upbringing to becoming a resilient young man had been transformative, filled with invaluable lessons and experiences that shaped him. As he reflected on his time at the National Institute of Technology (NIT), he felt a deep sense of gratitude for everything he had learned.

The Importance of Perseverance

One of the most crucial lessons Arjun learned at NIT was the importance of perseverance. The rigorous academic environment pushed him to his limits, demanding late nights and relentless dedication. There were moments when the workload seemed insurmountable, and the pressure felt overwhelming. But through these challenges, Arjun discovered that success often comes to those who refuse to give up.

Advice to Engineering Students:

- **Stay Committed:** No matter how tough the journey gets, remember that persistence is key. Keep pushing through, even when it feels like the odds are against you.
- **Set Small Goals:** Break down your larger goals into manageable tasks. Celebrate small victories along the way to keep yourself motivated.

Building Lifelong Friendships

The friendships Arjun formed at NIT became the cornerstone of his college experience. Suresh, Kavya, and Rajat were more than just friends; they were his support system. Together, they navigated the highs and lows of college life, forming bonds that would last a lifetime. These relationships provided emotional support, laughter, and shared memories that made the journey worthwhile.

Advice to Engineering Students:

- **Value Your Friendships:** The friends you make during your college years can become your lifelong allies. Invest time in building and nurturing these relationships.
- **Lean on Each Other:** Don't hesitate to seek support from your friends during tough times. Sharing your struggles can make the burden easier to bear.

The Power of Adaptability

Arjun's involvement in various extracurricular activities taught him the power of adaptability. From volunteering to founding an electrical engineering club, he learned to navigate different roles and responsibilities. These experiences broadened his horizons, teaching him leadership, teamwork, and the importance of giving back to the community.

Advice to Engineering Students:

- **Get Involved:** Participate in clubs, societies, and extracurricular activities. These experiences can help you develop essential skills and expand your network.
- **Be Open to New Experiences:** Embrace opportunities to step out of your comfort zone. Adaptability is a valuable trait that will serve you well in both personal and professional life.

Navigating Relationships

Arjun's experiences with relationships, both romantic and platonic, were integral to his personal growth. The late-night chats, the excitement of first love, the pain of heartbreak, and the eventual growth from these experiences shaped him into a more empathetic and emotionally intelligent person.

Advice to Engineering Students:

- **Prioritize Communication:** Whether in friendships or romantic relationships, clear and honest communication is crucial. Misunderstandings can be avoided with open dialogue.
- **Learn from Heartbreak:** Every relationship, whether it lasts or not, teaches you something valuable. Embrace these lessons and use them to grow.

Embracing Failure and Rejection

The placement season was one of the most challenging times for Arjun. Despite his strong profile, he faced multiple rejections, which took a toll on his mental health. However, seeking help from the campus counselling centre and relying on the support of his friends helped him navigate this tough period. His eventual success in securing a position at Rockwell Corporation was a testament to the importance of resilience and patience.

Advice to Engineering Students:

- **Don't Fear Failure:** Rejections and failures are part of the journey. Learn from them and use them as stepping stones to future success.
- **Seek Support:** Don't hesitate to seek help when you need it. Whether it's from friends, family, or professional counsellors, support systems are essential.

Transitioning to Professional Life

The shift from student life to professional life brought new challenges for Arjun. The steep learning curve, new responsibilities, and the need to adapt quickly were daunting. However, the lessons he had learned at NIT – perseverance, adaptability, and resilience – proved invaluable. With the support of his mentor and team, Arjun found his footing and began to thrive in his new role.

Advice to Engineering Students:

- **Embrace the Learning Curve:** The transition to professional life can be challenging, but it's also an opportunity to learn and grow. Be open to new experiences and continue to develop your skills.
- **Build a Support Network:** Seek mentors and build relationships with colleagues. A strong support network can provide guidance and help you navigate your career.

Cherishing Memories and Looking Forward

As Arjun reflected on his journey, he felt a profound sense of gratitude for the experiences and memories he had made at NIT. The lessons he had learned and the friendships he had formed were invaluable.

These experiences had prepared him for the challenges ahead and had shaped him into the person he was today.

Advice to Engineering Students:

- **Savour the Moment:** College years are unique and precious. Make the most of your time, create lasting memories, and cherish every moment.
- **Stay Connected:** Maintain the friendships and connections you make. These relationships can provide support and joy throughout your life.

Moving Forward with Confidence

With a heart full of hope and a mind ready for new adventures, Arjun was prepared to face whatever lay ahead. The experiences and achievements of his time at NIT were just the beginning. The future was bright, and he was ready to embrace it with confidence and excitement.

Final Words of Advice to Engineering Students:

- **Stay Resilient:** Life will have its ups and downs. Stay resilient, adapt to changes, and keep moving forward.
- **Believe in Yourself:** Trust in your abilities and have confidence in the journey ahead. Your experiences have prepared you well for the challenges to come.

As Arjun turned away from the window and prepared for the next day, he felt a sense of peace. The journey had been long and winding, but it had made him who he was today – a resilient, confident, and determined young man, ready to take on the world. The experiences at NIT had been a crucial part of his journey, and the lessons he had learned would stay with him forever.

Arjun Mehra stepped into the future with a heart full of gratitude and a mind ready for new adventures. The journey from a pampered boy to a resilient young man had been transformative, and he was prepared to face the world with confidence and determination. The lessons of perseverance, adaptability, and resilience would continue to guide him, and the friendships he had formed would always be a source of strength and support.

About the Author

Swagat Mohanty

Swagat Mohanty is an accomplished professional with a rich educational and professional background. He holds an MBA from HEC Paris, a globally renowned business school, and a B.Tech from the National Institute of Technology (NIT) Rourkela, one of India's leading engineering institutions.

With six years of experience in the financial industry, Swagat has held significant roles at prestigious firms such as JP Morgan and Fidelity Investments.

In addition to his corporate experience, Swagat has demonstrated his entrepreneurial spirit by running his own social impact startup for three years. Swagat has also been actively involved in the venture capital sector, working with various venture capital funds.

Beyond his professional pursuits, Swagat is a passionate writer. His first book, "Tangled Syllables," is a collection of poems that reflects his literary talent and creative passion.

www.ingramcontent.com/pod-product-compliance
Lightning Source LLC
LaVergne TN
LVHW041607070526
838199LV00052B/3025